STOLEN DESTINY

THIEF OF HEARTS

C.R. JANE

MILA YOUNG

CONTENTS

What is a siren without her power?

I'm about to find out, and I have no problems embracing the darkness to do so.

I was thrown into a literal hell, and every day feels like it could be my last.

But amid such darkness, I thought I found light with three men who've shown me happiness is possible even in a place like this.

But maybe I was too quick to trust and give my heart away.

They say trust takes years to build, seconds to break... and I don't think forever will be long enough to repair what they did to me.

One will sacrifice himself for me. One will shatter my soul.And one will kill me to save me.

Enjoy your stay at Nightmare Penitentiary. Death is only a matter of time.

CHAPTER 1

ALARIC

She was fucking acting like I didn't exist

It had been days since Selena even looked me in the eyes during her food deliveries.

At first, I was amused, but now…I was just annoyed.

"Lose your tongue again today, Luv?" I asked sarcastically as she once again dropped a tray of food on the floor in front of me, not seeming to care that her actions had led to half of the slop they were serving today ending up out of the tray.

Silence.

Well that wouldn't do. I shifted on my bed, making sure that my abs were accentuated with the movement. I knew Selena loved my body. The hot as fuck, best sex of my life with her was evidence of that.

Nothing. Not even a blush to that gorgeous face of hers.

What. The. Fuck.

I wondered how long she was going to be able to

ignore me like this. I couldn't believe she was holding it against me that I didn't help her with her little favor.

If she thought I was going to waste a shot at the warden's treasure for the angst ridden fae she seemed to have a soft spot for suddenly…she had lost her mind.

When I took my shot at the warden, it would be while I was getting out of here, with hopefully Selena by my side.

Hmm, that was new. I had never pictured any woman by my side in any capacity. I preferred them to be under me or spread out before me as I feasted on them, and then gone, permanently.

I twitched uncomfortably at the direction my thoughts were going of Selena by my side in a permanent way.

I was an incubus, my whole being was designed to procure me pleasure. I had never been one to not get what I wanted, nor did I have patience for anything but that. If the incubus inside of me had decided that Selena was going to be in my life for more than the brief, if extremely pleasurable, interludes we'd thus far had together, I wasn't going to argue.

A burning started in my chest, not necessarily painful, but uncomfortable. It took me a second to place what the feeling was. When I peered down at my chest, I reared back in shock, a solitary rose tattoo was imprinted in the center of my chest.

A mating symbol.

They were different for every incubus, designed to reflect the trait of their mate rather than the incubus.

I'd never seen one in person, only heard about it, but incubi weren't really ones to settle down or even want to settle down after all.

Evidently, my imprisonment had allowed my mate bond to link with Selena. That, and the several times we'd fucked.

Fuck.

My mate was fucking ignoring me.

That wasn't going to work.

Fuck that.

* * *

I heard Selena's food cart long before she came into view. Even the sound had my groin hardening painfully. I now got erections from hearing a food cart. Perfect.

A few moments later, she came into view, looking ridiculously perfect despite the fact that the prison jumpsuit she had on didn't do anyone any favors.

I waited for a second for her to acknowledge me, my insides dipping when she didn't even give me a look.

"Did you bring me something good today, sweetheart?" I goaded. What I was feeling today went far beyond annoyance. I was furious. How dare she ignore me. I didn't want to have a mate. I didn't want to be tied down, especially when it meant that I would need to be getting two people out of this hellhole instead of just myself.

Deciding I'd had enough, I let out a burst of power. It wouldn't send her into an orgasm, but it would get her attention.

Except it didn't. I didn't even get a fucking tell-tale blush to her cheeks.

Not thinking, I sent another burst of power at her as she bent down to throw my tray on the ground. Preparing myself for her to throw herself at me, I stood up from my bed and leaned against the wall.

Nothing. Just a faint twitch of irritation, as if I had pushed her instead of sent a straight shot of lust at her.

Feeling irrationally desperate, I unloaded another spray of power, something that would normally send anyone in the vicinity into a sexual free fall for the next week. The guard that had been with her had already disappeared, I'm sure to fuck the first thing in sight.

He would hate himself in the morning.

I could hear my companions in the cells on both sides of me jerking off, their breaths heavy as they mindlessly rutted against their hands, desperate for relief.

But all Selena did was give me a dirty look, as if she knew what I was trying to do.

But she couldn't know.

I'd never met a creature alive who was immune to my powers. Even the warden himself wouldn't be able to ignore me on the day that I decided to leave this place. I was actually looking forward to what I had planned for him.

But here she was, walking out of my cell like she

didn't have a care in the fucking world, not showing a sign of lust.

I sniffed the air, desperate for that telltale sweet smell of her arousal that drove me crazy.

Nothing.

My heart beat madly in my chest. I felt desperate. I felt delirious. I felt crazed.

Who was this woman, and what magic did she possess to be able to block me?

Her stalker guard appeared just then, his eyes intent on her. He was always watching her. I wondered if Selena knew just how much.

I hated him. Another surprising thing, as I had never felt anything close to jealousy over a woman before. Selena turned, giving him the smile that I was desperate to have directed at me.

She pulled him towards her, giving him a kiss that looked to be only partly aimed at getting back at me. She still didn't look at me as she pulled away from him. Her idiot stalker looked like he was going to keel over from her touch.

Maybe he would die and I would be saved the trouble later, because one thing was for sure.

Selena was mine.

CHAPTER 2

SELENA

I must have been doing better than I thought at pretending to ignore Alaric, because I could feel the anger radiating off of him as days passed and I continued to ignore his presence.

It was the furthest thing from the truth though. Everything about him called to me. My whole body vibrated with the need to have him touch me. I gave myself a daily pep talk before my meal duties that I would continue to pretend like he didn't exist.

I was nothing to him. Just a hole he'd plugged with his dick a few times. If I meant anything to him, he would have helped me the other day when I'd asked. It was common knowledge that Alaric could do anything and get anything he wanted down here.

A maddening voice in my head reminded me that someone like Alaric would only bring me heartache.

I grudgingly dragged myself down a hallway, unable to get him out of my mind. I've never met anyone with so much pride that it shocked him when I didn't fall into line and serve him. I did, however, love every second of watching his expression fall when I refused his allure. Guess it wasn't everyday someone walked away unscathed from an incubus. He'd called to me the first time that I saw him in his cell, and it hadn't gotten any better when he swept in like a storm to the prison kitchen and claimed me then and there. I had no idea what was going on and fell for his charm. I had sex with him on the counter where anyone could walk in on us, and he gloated afterwards.

Asshole.

Wankhammer.

Douche.

I gritted my teeth as I stormed forward, ignoring the hoots and screams from other inmates in their cells.

I might have been a sucker with Alaric before, but after finding out what he was, the tables had turned. Information was key and knowing he was an incubus made it easier to resist him…especially for a siren like me. And after that little encounter with him, I intended to use every bit in my favor and see how he enjoyed being played.

The communal section of the penitentiary buzzed with activity. Prisoners chatted, played ping pong or cards, but I marched right past them and into the empty cafeteria. The tables and seats were clean, and on the counter, the only food that remained were five Styrofoam cups with leftover corn soup from the last meal. Gross, but I still took one, as it was the equivalent of me searching my fridge for anything to snack on when I got upset. I sat in the corner on my own, needing to breathe and calm my thoughts.

I took a sip and chewed on the corn kernels. Even if I hated this soup, I ended up finishing it all, and even glanced over my shoulder for another helping.

"You can't be here alone," a guard snapped from the doorway. "Head back to your cell."

I sucked in a raspy breath, frustration worming its way through my veins, and I climbed to my feet. I missed the freedom to just be left alone.

After the guard chased me out of the cafeteria, I dragged myself down the corridor, not wanting to return to my cell. Not when my mind refused to stop overthinking Alaric's arrogance.

I'd been strolling for the past fifteen minutes, my head low, passing other inmates. Before I realized it, I'd walked directly toward Seth's cell. The metal door swung open, missing my face by inches.

I lurched backward, my heart banging in my chest as I backed away just as the warden stepped out. His intense gaze swept in my direction, burrowing into me, reminding me of our little deal in his office over Seth.

If you succeed, I will give you back your power. Then he proceeded to gaze over to the shelf where he kept a golden orb that contained my essence.

My gut clenched at the memory.

Win over his confidence, he'd said. *Find out where he*

put his father's scepter. It was hidden after the murder. The light fae can't appoint a new king without it.

His command stayed with me, as did his final promise if I failed. He'd add an extra ten years to my sentence. A shiver curled up my spine at the thought. I didn't even know if I could last a year, let alone ten in this place.

The warden held onto the open metal door with one hand, his gaze weighing heavily on me. He was wearing the brown leather coat he seemed to wear everywhere. It fell to his knees and gaped open, revealing black pants and a clean white button-up shirt underneath. I was guessing he didn't get his hands dirty when he ordered others to do his work. Considering he'd just come out of Seth's room, his visit would have been anything but pleasant.

I blinked, unsure if my eyes were blurry or if I was really seeing thin tendrils of smoke curling away from his body. So many rumors talked about what the warden was...though no one seemed to know... I suspected he might have some affinity with demons. He may have looked young and very easy on the eyes, but he wasn't a man anyone should trust.

He leaned in closer.

"Selena," he barked my name, corded muscles tensing in his neck. One word was all he gave me, but there was enough warning behind it to leave me shuddering.

I nodded once, while my ears filled with the sound of my panicked heart.

The warden straightened, cracked his neck, and moved aside to give me room to pass him into Seth's cell. The warning came again in his gaze.

I moved quickly and slid past him, my skin crawling. Then I turned into the cell, where a guard waited outside.

Without a word, I slipped inside cautiously, unsure what to expect.

Last time I'd spoken with Seth, he was furious, unhinged, and in truth, I'm more scared of the guards beating him again if he doesn't control himself.

I swallowed past my dried throat, my gaze frantically scanning the dimly lit cell. They landed on the figure lying on the bed. There was a plastic crate nearby him, probably used as a seat. The toilet and sink were against the back wall, like in all our cells, and a shelf unit with clothes and a few books were the only pieces in here.

My stomach twisted on itself, because me being here was a terrible idea and I hated being put in this situation. What I loathed worse was that I gave Seth's crystal to the warden. Had I known, I would never have done that.

I took slow steps forward and stopped at the foot of his bed.

He was lying on his back, eyes closed, his orange jumpsuit rolled down to his waist, his chest and arms covered in healed and fresh wounds. They overlapped each other like a macabre puzzle that told the story of torture and sorrow.

My breaths smothered in my lungs to see him this way. Seth was a strong, muscular fae, his gorgeous face pale and his lips dry. My heart went out to him at his treatment. I'd welcome death if I were him, rather than keep living with these daily beatings.

I didn't dare step any closer to him, and instead, I gripped the metal railing at the foot of his bed, chewing on my inner lip. I glanced over my shoulder to the door where the shadow of a guard remained. They waited, probably listening.

"Dana," Seth croaked.

I swung back around and stiffened, having no clue who Dana was. Could she be his wife or sister back in the fae realm?

"Is that you?" He titled his head up, eyes squinting in my direction, and for those few moments, a fae with hope and kindness lay before me. I wanted to remain quiet and make time stand still for him. To bring him some semblance of peace, because whoever Dana was, she had to be important if she was the first name that came to his mind.

When I didn't respond, he squinted past the shadows. "Who are you?"

"It's me, Selena," I answered, my insides squeezing at how he'd respond.

He groaned and dropped his head back to the mattress.

Well, on the bright side, he hadn't screamed at me yet.

I found my bravery and moved over to the side of

his bed and dragged the seat out of arm's reach. It made a horrible screeching sound, and I cringed.

Seth huffed, his nostrils flaring, as if it took every inch of strength he had left to not yell at me.

I flopped down onto the seat, pressed my knees together, and put my hands in my lap. My mind ran over what I should say.

Hey, how are you doing, was out of the question. So was, *the slop at the cafeteria sucks,* since I'd never seen him there. Gods, I was horrible at this. The warden expected me to sweet talk information out of Seth, yet I couldn't even form an initial sentence. This was going to go down in flames, and I'd burn in this hellhole for the next ten years.

"What do you want?" he snarled.

Okay, I could work with that conversation opener.

"I wanted to check on you."

"Don't lie. Nobody checks on anyone in this place without a motive." He groaned as he strained to turn onto his side. "What's yours?"

I shifted uncomfortably, convinced I couldn't do this. He'd suffered enough, so who was I to take from him whatever secret he held onto? I didn't trust the warden, yet he promised me powers. Disobey him, and I would be stuck here. But when I looked into Seth's pale blue eyes, at the agony in his face, my heart bled. Maybe I didn't need to make that decision now.

He stared at me, waiting for my response. "Guilt," I admitted, which was partially the truth.

His eyes never left me. "Are you alleviated yet of

your guilt so you can sleep better at night?" His spite-fulness didn't surprise me, but it also grated on my nerves.

"Fine, you're upset with me, but I never meant to take your crystal away," I whispered.

He rolled onto his back. "Just leave."

My insides squeezed as guilt ate away at me. Instead of being here to help the warden, I ought to find a way to aid Seth. Maybe that was the better option.

I stood when I noticed the cut on his bicep, blood rolling over his arm and onto the blanket underneath him. He didn't seem to notice or care.

I glanced around and a small towel near the sink caught my attention. With quick steps, I grabbed the towel and soaked a corner before wringing out excess water.

Three strides took me to his side, and I pulled the chair so I sat closer to his bed. "Will you let me clean your wound?" I ask.

He stared at me, his brow furrowed, and I expected the worst. It took him a long pause to respond, which came in the form of a nod. My fingers lay gently over his bicep while I patted away the blood with the damp cloth. He flinched at my touch, and I paused. "Sorry."

How long had they been torturing him that a small tender touch made him react in such a way? Gingerly, I continued, and he let out a pain-filled groan when I did cleanse his cut.

With the dry end of the fabric, I pressed it to the injury, helping to stop the bleeding and allow the blood to coagulate. Though I understood little about fae anatomy to know if their blood worked the same way as mine and what I was doing would actually help.

I wiped more dried blood from his forearm and even the side of his waist with soft strokes.

His lips thinned, gaze still on me. The stale air in the room wrapped its arms around me, and the metallic smell of blood teased my nostrils. I looked down to the blanket over the mattress, stained with too much blood. Seth and I were strangers, forced together out of pure accident, and every inch of me screamed to get out of here. Yet a sliver in my heart hurt to witness such brutality against him.

"Seth, I'm really sorry I took the crystal." The faint words escaped my lips again as I bowed my head down and cleaned him.

No response.

When he didn't answer, I asked, "Who is Dana?"

He never answered and closed his eyes instead. I wiped more dried blood from him, feeling like some of this might be from a day or two ago.

"Why are you in here?" I asked an obvious question, changing the topic of conversation, hoping it might get him to talk.

"My father," was all he said. No indication if he had killed him or that he was framed.

Silence followed.

I looked over to the door and the guard's shadow no longer lingered. Though I doubted he'd be far. Instead of leaving, I remained by Seth's side and kept him company. I stared at his chest, the muscles under my towel as I wiped more dried blood away. He didn't deserve this.

They said he killed his father, the king, but when I studied his face, he didn't look like the killing kind. I almost laughed out loud at myself. How would I know what a killer looked like?

I mean, I ended up in this place, and I hadn't hurt a soul. Unless I counted Julian's ego. Fucking vampire asshole needed to rot in this penitentiary, not me.

The lines on Seth's face etched the story of a hard life, the light creases at the corners of his eyes spoke of stress. The story of sorrow was written over his face, and belonged to someone who had lost so much, it left him desolate. *So what is your story? Did you kill your father or are you protecting something or someone else?*

He was rugged, but heh ad ivory skin like he didn't spend a lot of time outdoors. Long silvery white hair spread out around his head, bits stained by blood from his shoulders.

The more I studied him, the more I struggled to believe he would kill his father. I felt it in my gut, in my bones, in my soul.

His breaths grew heavy and deep, and it wasn't long before he'd fallen asleep. If my company had brought him peace for a short while, then I'd be satisfied my visit didn't bring him more tension.

A speck of blood stained his cheek, and I reached over to scrub it away when his hand clasped my wrist.

I jumped in my skin, stiffening all over.

He drew my hand to his chest where he held it. He still slept though, his exhales long and raspy. "Stay with me," he murmured under his breath.

I didn't move. His hand looked so much bigger than mine, his fingers curled around mine, like holding me was the most cherished thing in his world.

Agony choked me that such a powerful fae had been broken down to where his mind retreated to the past. How long before he couldn't distinguish between present and past? How far would the warden keep pushing this fae? At this rate, he'd kill Seth before he gained the information he needed on the scepter.

The air suddenly turned bitter and chilled my skin as a shadow fell over the room. I lifted my chin to find the guard standing in the doorway.

Looking back at Seth, he looked so peaceful, so I tenderly removed my hand from under his touch and climbed to my feet. On soft steps, I left his cell. The guard backed away as I stepped out, then he shut the door with a bang, making as much noise as he possibly could.

Asshole. I seriously hated the guards and the warden more and more with each passing day.

I turned away from him and made my way back toward my cell. My throat thickened each time I remembered the sorrowful look on Seth's face, the layers of wounds. What was being done to him sickened me.

Inmates passed me, some knocked their shoulders into me on purpose as I passed. I ignored their attempts to start a fight. I'd seen enough to know how people in this penitentiary dealt with boredom.

I rushed forward, and all I could think about was Seth. My eyes stung with tears. By the time I reached my cell, I darted inside and threw myself into my bed. Hugging my pillow, I curled in on myself and the tears fell.

Torment ripped through me, and as much I told myself to be strong, to not take on other people's feelings, I failed miserably. My heart kept shattering over and over at seeing how far they had broken Seth.

CHAPTER 3

SELENA

"Get up!" a gruff voice barked, stirring me from a fitful slumber. It had taken me forever to fall asleep last night, and I didn't appreciate being woken up early. That was about the only thing you could count on in this hellhole—there was a schedule that was rigidly kept.

I reluctantly opened my eyes, but evidently, I wasn't quick enough. A bucket of filthy, ice-cold water was flung on me, soaking my entire body and my bed. I sat up, sputtering. I was furious enough to leap out of bed and toward the guard leering at me from the foot of my bed. My hands curled up into claws as I strained to hold myself back from ripping into his.

The smug-looking blond guard held my gaze, just daring me to attack him. Taking a deep, shaky breath, I tried to come down from the bolt of adrenaline coursing through my body at my rude awakening. I schooled my features into what hopefully looked like a blank face.

The guard's face dropped. Evidently, he was looking for a fight this morning. Just like every jerk living under this roof.

"Can I help you?" I asked coldly, trying to act dignified as I shivered there in my soaking wet bed. I didn't even want to know what was in the water he'd just thrown at me, or where it had come from. It stunk so bad, my eyes were watering.

"You have a visitor. You have five minutes to get yourself together, and then we're going..." He paused for dramatic affect. "No matter what you're wearing."

The gleam in his eye told me he hoped that I was wearing nothing at that point.

The second he stepped out of view of my cell—although I was sure he was hovering right outside of the periphery, watching my every move like the perv I knew that he was—I sprang from my bed, rushing to the rusty sink in the corner, my mind racing as I thought about who my visitor could be. In the time that I had been here, I hadn't had a single one, not that I was expecting one really, so this was quite the surprise.

Turning on the faucet, I collected the water in my hands and tried to give myself a hasty bath. After a few useless splashes across my face, I stopped my efforts. It was most likely Julian here to gloat. He was the person I cared the least about impressing.

It would probably make him delighted to see me

like this. Maybe he would forget all about punishing me because he wouldn't want me anymore.

Of course, him wanting me was probably the only way I was going to get out of here. My stream of thoughts were interrupted by the guard marching into the cell and grabbing my arm. I guess my five minutes were up.

I'm sure I looked like a drowned rat as he dragged me out into the hallway, but at least my smell was keeping him from groping me. His face was scrunched up in disgust, and he looked a little green around the gills from being this close to me.

Maybe I should start dumping that sludge on me every day to serve as some sort of repellant to the rest of the prison population. The little smile on my face seemed to infuriate the guard, because he made sure that he scraped me against the stone wall a few times.

My smile faded quickly after I started bleeding. I would probably get some sort of deadly disease from having open wounds in my current state of filth.

I was a painful mess once we got to a part of the prison I'd never been to before. The guard waved his hand in front of the door, and it opened. I could almost hear him saying some sort of spell in his head as it did so.

The guard's antagonistic scowl faded quickly the second we stepped into the non-descript grey room that I quickly realized must have been the visitor's room, based on the tables set up around the room filled with prisoners in jumpsuits and normal dressed people.

I knew why the guard's attitude had changed as soon I saw her sitting there.

It was my mother.

Fuck.

Rosalind looked as beautiful as ever, if a little more gaunt than I remembered her looking before. Her face didn't change as she surveyed me, it was a cool mask, the kind of look that I'd been trying my hardest to adopt during my stay at Nightmare Penitentiary. She pulled it off far better than I did. You could barely see the disgust over my appearance in her eyes.

That alone got my hackles up. To the rest of the world, she might be like ice, but with me, she had never bothered to hide before how much she hated me.

The guard's grip on me loosened as he adopted what I was sure he thought was an attractive swagger as he led me to the table where my mother was sitting.

"Ma'am," he tried to say seductively as he did a little nod with his head.

I snorted, and he shot me a look of rage that promised that my trip back to my cell would be even worse than the one I'd just experienced.

"Thank you, Officer," my mother cooed in that affected voice that had always sent her suitors and clients swooning.

This time, I resisted laughing at her use of the word "officer." I didn't want to die on the trip back.

The guard stood there staring at my mother silently

for a long, awkward moment as Rosalind turned her attention back to me. It was a bad habit of mine that her interest immediately made me doubt everything about myself. It was like she had the power to peel back the layers of my skin to unleash every insecurity I'd ever had in my life. Although I guess she knew where to look for them. She had been the one to give me all of them in the first place, after all.

"Do you think I could have a minute with my daughter?" Rosalind asked in that same breathy voice. The guard literally seemed to melt into a puddle next to me.

"Of course," he answered quickly. "I'll just be right over there if you need me," he said, pointing to the wall where a few other guards were standing, surveying the room closely as they waited for any of the prisoners to step out of line.

I didn't bother looking around the room to see who else was in here, the most dangerous creature in the room was sitting across the table in front of me.

As soon as the guard had gone far enough away that he couldn't hear us, my mother's pleasant façade dropped.

"I can see this place isn't doing you any favors," she sneered, her lip curling up in disgust. I kept my spine straight as I attempted to let her cruel words bounce off me. I'd long ago stopped expecting, or wishing, that she was someone different. Rosalind was a pretty monster, she would never be anything else.

"Hello to you too, Rosalind," I replied calmly. I

dragged my gaze off her, staring at my dirt ridden nails as if they were suddenly the most interesting thing I'd ever seen.

"You need to beg Julian for forgiveness. I don't care what it takes, if you need to offer your virginity on a silver platter—" she began, cutting off suddenly by the way my face must have twitched at her use of the word "virginity."

Her face almost looked panicked. "You didn't," she seethed in a voice laden with fear and hatred. "You stupid, stupid girl. You might have ruined us all."

"What's going on?" I asked, neither confirming nor denying her suspicion about my V-card.

My mother looked frazzled at the question. She looked frail in that moment, like whatever Julian was doing was so terrible that it had crushed her spirit.

I didn't feel sorry for her. I wasn't capable of that after everything she'd done to me and every other innocent girl under her care.

"He's gone mad," she hissed urgently, leaning towards me as her hands clenched at the table like she was holding herself back from grabbing me. "He's killed five of my girls just in the last week."

My heart dropped. I may have hated my mother, but most of the girls were like me, victims of the vampires' tyranny. "Why?" I asked in shock. Julian had always been a cruel taskmaster, but he knew that his siren sex workers were priceless. He never would have done anything actually fatal to them in the past.

She pulled away and studied me again. "We aren't

sure. But it happened in the days after he brought you here. There are rumors that he's become addicted to you and his violent mood swings are some sort of withdrawal." She huffed as if that was the most ridiculous thing she'd ever heard.

"Was he feeding off you?" she suddenly asked in disgust.

I scowled at her. That right there was proof of the kind of mother she had been to me. She was disgusted at the idea of me letting Julian feed off me rather than worried and upset about the fact that he could have been feeding off her underage daughter right under her nose.

"No, he wasn't," I answered coldly. She stared at me as if she didn't believe me.

"He probably just has some business deal that's gone bad or something," I offered unhelpfully.

I tried not to flinch in front of the hate she wore on her face as she looked at me. It was difficult for me to comprehend how you could carry someone inside of you, be there when they came into creation, and then hate them forever after that.

"Listen, you little bitch," she seethed, trying to keep her features calm in the face of the guards who were watching us. "This is what you're going to do. I'm going to get you a meeting with Julian. And then you are going to beg on your hands and knees for his forgiveness, give him whatever he wants, and make him happy again. Or I'm going to make sure you rot in this place for the rest of your existence."

I tilted my chin up, rage surging through me that she would dare make any requests from me after everything she'd put me through in my life. Maybe Nightmare Penitentiary needed to change its name, because compared to the prospect of a lifetime of servitude to her and Julian, I would take my dank cell, the abusive guards, the threats, and the shitty food.

At least I was having hot sex.

"You can go to hell," I told her with a smirk, savoring the way her face fell in disbelief. Her mouth moved like a fish as she struggled to form words.

"What did you just say?" she screeched, causing every eye in the room to turn towards us. Frantically, she smoothed her hair and tried to put a pleasant smile on her lips, even though her hands were shaking from trying to control herself. If we were alone, she'd have already flung herself at me, trying to inflict as much bodily harm as possible.

I leaned forward, my lips curling mockingly. "I said, there's no fucking way that I would ever help you out, you fucking cunt."

I've never spoken like this to my mother. In fact, I couldn't really remember a time when I'd ever been anything less than respectful of her. This felt freeing. Powerful. Fucking fantastic.

One of Rosalind's eyes twitched from the effort of holding herself back. My mother had always prized herself on her control, but it looked like I was pushing that control to the very edge.

She stood up slowly, her hands shaking beside her.

"You're going to regret this day, little girl," she warned in a throaty growl. She finally couldn't hold herself back, and she reared back her hand and slapped me in the face. My head flew back with the impact, but I kept myself silent, determined not to give her the satisfaction of hearing evidence of my pain.

Now everyone was really watching us, and I saw a few guards step forward, looking unsure of what to do. My asshole of a blond guard made some kind of gesture, and they all stepped back and relaxed.

Typical.

I rolled my eyes, gesturing around me as I ignored the pain pulsating from my cheek. "I highly doubt that," I told her haughtily, remaining seated with my chin held high.

She didn't know what to do with me. The rage and confusion were more than she could take. Figuring I might as well go all the way, I spit at her while flipping her off, enjoying the gasps of shock from some of the family members at other tables. The prisoners I could see just looked impressed. Her hand flew to her cheek where a blob of spittle was displayed. She wiped it off, staring at the evidence of my insurrection in her hand in disbelief.

Her mouth hung open, and once again, she was at a loss for words.

When it was evident that I wasn't going to change my mind, and before she had to endure any more public displays of humiliation, she whirled away and left the room through the back entrance without a look back.

I was trembling slightly as I stood there. I kind of couldn't believe that I'd just done that. I'd spent whole days over the years going through in my mind what I would say to her if I was braver, what I would do.

Who knew that being sent to the prison of everyone's nightmares would finally make me brave enough to say some of those things?

I felt a twinge of guilt about the girls Rosalind had said Julian was hurting. What if I could have helped them by giving in?

No sooner did the thought pass through my mind, then I quickly reminded myself that Rosalind was a master manipulator and Julian was even worse. No matter what I did, the sirens wouldn't be free. No matter what I did, Julian wouldn't change.

The guard appeared by my side, startling me since I'd still been staring at the doorway that Rosalind just disappeared behind.

I felt...complicated. While my initial emotions were pride and satisfaction, my adrenaline was fading and now I felt shaky. Shaky...and alone.

Although I had long ago come to terms with the fact that Rosalind was more likely to kill me than to help me, there was something about seeing your mother turn their back on you. The feeling of loneliness that came from that was a hard thing to shake, especially when my blond tormentor appeared next to me, a savage grin on his face at what he'd just witnessed go down between Rosalind and myself.

"You're really livening up the place," he commented, a sadistic sparkle in his eye that promised he had plans for me as soon as we left this room.

I sighed and accepted my fate that whatever he had planned for me was going to be extremely unenjoyable. But I'd lived through all the other shit in my life, I would live through whatever he had planned for me as well.

Probably.

He led me with a firm grip on my arm out of the room. I could feel all the occupant's gazes on me as I left. At least their stares were more likely related to my wet dog look, terrible smell, and the fight I'd just had with Rosalind, rather than any residual siren power. Once again, I thought about rocking this look more often.

We rounded a corner and ran right into a harried-looking Keon, who looked like he'd just finished sprinting. His gaze grew hard as he looked at the way the guard was gripping my arm tightly. When he saw how bad I looked, and the blossoming bruise on my cheek, his gaze hardened even more.

"I'll take the prisoner from here," he growled at the idiot next to me.

Blondie puffed up his chest and took a threatening step towards Keon. Keon growled, and his eyes seemed to take on a glow, something I hadn't seen happen with him before. The guard immediately stepped back, his body trembling in fear. I looked at him quizzically, not sure that Keon's growl warranted such a reaction. The guard's eyes flicked towards me.

"Don't look at her," Keon snarled, and the guard's eyes immediately went to the ground. The scent of urine assaulted me as the guard pissed his pants.

What. The. Hell?

"Get out of here," Keon ordered, and the guard immediately left, practically at a run. I turned to look at Keon in confusion.

"What was that?" I asked, but I only said it half-heartedly, because after my little interaction with my mother, I couldn't find it in me to care that much. I was just grateful that I wasn't going to deal with whatever horror fest that guard had planned on top of that.

"Hey, you okay?" Keon asked softly, ignoring my question. His voice was a complete one-eighty from the way that he had barked at the guard.

"Perfect," I said, but again, my words don't have any real force behind them.

Keon wrapped his arm around my waist and began to lead me down the hall. I realized belatedly that we were going the opposite way from my cell. I didn't say anything. I just let him lead me wherever he wanted to go. Maybe I shouldn't have trusted him so easily, so soon. But I did.

Or maybe it wasn't trust, it was just that I felt numb right then after my encounter with Rosalind. And the presence of Keon usually meant that pleasure would follow.

And I needed all the pleasure I could get.

We encountered a few more guards as we walked, but they all kept their gazes averted from Keon as well. I hadn't noticed this reaction before, and I wondered what had changed, or maybe it had always been like this and I just hadn't been paying enough attention.

We finally got to his quarters, and I leaned against the wall with a sigh as he unlocked the door before I followed him inside.

Once we were cocooned inside, Keon tipped up my chin to face him. "What happened?"

I sighed and looked away from him. I'd never really realized before now how the fact that my own mother hated me messed with my head about how I was supposed to feel about myself.

"Just more of the same bullshit," I told him vaguely. Keon didn't know anything about my past, unless my prison file had something in it. I guessed it was the next step that we needed to take, talking about our pasts.

But I didn't feel like taking that step right now.

I just wanted him to make me forget.

"Can I use your shower?" I asked, not able to stand the smell of the rancid water a second longer.

"Of course," he said, showing me to the shower and where a towel was. He then left the room, something I was grateful for as I started to fall apart.

I stayed under the water for a long time, hoping it could wash away what I was feeling. But I only felt marginally better when I finally got out.

I stared at myself in the mirror above his sink, wondering about who I was and what I was becoming.

The door to the bathroom cracked open. Keon poked his head inside. "Are you alright?" he asked gently.

"Keon," I responded brokenly.

He flinched at the tears in my voice, closing his eyes like they were physically hurting him. He opened his eyes after a minute, resolution in his gaze.

"Get on the bed." It was a soft command, but a command all the same. I walked over to the bed in the next room, scooted to the middle of the mattress, and dropped from my elbows as he pulled his belt free. Need rushed between my thighs, and I welcomed the distraction.

Keon watched me squirm. One button, then the next, and by the time he freed his shirt and bared his chest, my clit was throbbing and I was wet, so wet, and panting with anticipation. His pants and boxer briefs followed. He stood stock still, hand stroking his hard length as I took in my fill. His abdomen rippled with dips and shadows.

Keon walked towards me, pinning me against the bed with the magnitude of his intense stare. His expression was more than hunger. It was filled with something I didn't want to put a name to, but that I wanted desperately.

Hot tears suddenly stung my eyes, blurring my vision as I attempted to fight them off. I didn't want to cry because of Rosalind. But dammit, it just felt nice that Keon seemed to care.

All I wanted in that moment was for him to kiss me. It hadn't been that long since our last kiss, but the prison had a way of making you forget everything good that happened in your life. Each day that passed might as well have been a year for how well it worked to push any good memories further and further away, like good moments in my life were nothing but a dream.

I realized then how much I was falling apart with everything that had happened lately, from Rosalind's visit, the warden's demands, the tension with Alaric, and the guilt I felt over Seth.

It felt like only Keon could save me in that moment.

"Stop thinking," he commanded. Naked, he stalked towards the bed, leaning over me as his hands found my hips. His fingers dug into my skin, as if he were holding tight and incapable of letting me go. My eyes closed. Tears streamed down my cheeks. A warmth against my lips, like the kind I yearned for when I was lonely in my cell, ignited a spark inside me.

He kissed me.

And the kiss was soft and tender, just what I needed right now.

His right hand left my side and trailed up to the side of my cheek, delicately cupping my face as his lips worked mine apart. Our tongues danced, and the taste of him set me on fire.

I craved him—his touch, his taste, his scent. I closed

my eyes, not sure what he would see in my gaze if I opened them. I felt too raw to show him that. Keon always saw too much.

Keon's left hand traveled down my side, pulling down the oversized prison pants I'd thrown on after my shower so that he could slip his hand between them and tug my panties to the side. One finger passed between my folds as he found the innermost part of me. He slipped one finger inside, followed by a second, curling them toward him and stroking me, long and gentle, slow and meaningful, as if he were trying to savor our connection. His fingers filled me while his lips went to work.

Doubt creeped in just then. What if Keon was a user just like everyone else I'd ever had in my life? None of this was real.

My mouth hung open, silently begging for him to quiet my thoughts with his lips. I knew it would work. If he kissed me, nothing else would matter, if only temporarily.

"I want you." I stared at the stained concrete floors next to the bed, still unwilling to admit that while looking him in the eyes. Admitting that much threatened to suck my life out of me.

Keon's hand angled under my jaw, lifting my mouth to his and breathing life back into my exhausted soul, one kiss at a time. Unapologetic emotion rained down on me as the heat of his body made all the problems waiting for me outside of these four walls fade away.

Keon removed his hand from my wetness and

ripped my clothes off. They were all soon in a pile on the floor, and his hands immediately traced my naked flesh as his tongue tasted my arousal on his fingers that had been inside of me.

Yes, this was what I needed.

My heart pounded hard in my chest. I just wanted the emptiness to go away. I wanted to feel every inch of him inside me. The sensation of his hand grabbing his erection and positioning it at my entrance as my legs gripped his sides sent an ache straight to my core. But the second he entered me, the heavy, burdening pain dissipated into thin air. Like it was never there in the first place. With my arms draped over his shoulders, I gave myself to him.

The raw awareness of him moving inside of me made every thrust a thousand times more intense than I ever dreamed possible. I wanted the pleasure he could give me more than anything, and my body was willing to do whatever it needed to get it. My teeth grazed over my bottom lip as I stifled a moan. I didn't want to look at him. I didn't want to know if he was looking at me with deep longing or scarier…love.

It felt like love, the way he was fucking me, but it was easier to not get my hopes up if I didn't have to see his face.

My lower back arched as every thrust moved me up farther on the bed. His fingers were gripping my hips painfully, in a way I knew would leave bruises.

But it didn't matter. The physical pain on the outside was miniscule compared to what was going on inside me. My body and heart worked in tandem to soak in every detail of that moment, from the smell of the cologne that faintly floated from his sweat-glistened skin, to the way his hair felt as I gripped the back of his neck. My mind quieted itself, as if to graciously give me a break finally. Keon groaned as he released himself inside me, and I let go, riding an intense wave of all-consuming pleasure as my hips bucked wildly in response to his writhing cock. When it was all over, he pulled out of me and I rolled to my side, bringing my knees up to my chest in silent pain.

I needed someone, or something, to cling to before I crumpled. I forced my eyes open, looking at him finally. I drank him in, letting his beautiful gaze stare right into my soul.

He was real. He was there. He'd just made love to me. I don't think I could call it anything else. Even now, he was looking at me like I was everything.

I felt shy under his gaze. I opened my mouth to try and say something, anything to break this intense silence, but my ankle began to burn again like it had after the last time we'd had sex. Looking down at it, trying to rub the pain away, I was shocked to see another star appearing on my skin.

I looked at it and then him in confusion, but he just had a proud, satisfied look in his eyes as he stared down it.

The pain finally stopped, and I flopped back on the bed in confusion and exhaustion. This place was turning me inside out. Every day was something unexpected. I glanced at Keon again as he grabbed a cloth and wet it in the bathroom before bringing it over to me and cleaning me off. I blushed at the gesture. It felt so intimate, more intimate than what we'd just done felt like.

He set the cloth on the nightstand next to the bed and then laid down next to me, enveloping me in his arms once again.

"Sleep," he told me softly. "I'm right here. I'll always be right here."

My last thought as I drifted off to troubled dreams was if his statement applied to just his presence in the prison while I was here...or if he was talking about forever.

CHAPTER 4

SELENA

My skin tingled when I woke up, my thighs aching in a delicious way, and Keon was on my mind. He had this way of showing up when I needed him most. Whether I realized it or not at that moment, it became clear afterward. He swept me out of the horrid existence in this penitentiary for long enough to find my peace of mind. Now, all I could think about were his strong arms around me and that in his embrace, I could breathe in this place that suffocated me.

I rolled over in bed to find myself back in my cell, not Keon's quarters. I remembered closing my eyes, and I must have fallen asleep. I'd like one day to wake up in his bed with him…except this wasn't a fairy tale, now was it?

The small moments of escape he provided were everything to me—they were pockets of stepping out of my horrible situation.

I remained on my back and stared up at the stark white ceiling. My thoughts drifted to my mother's visit yesterday, and bitterness rose through me once more.

I had always been a good girl growing up. I listened to my mother, because that was the only life I'd known for so long.

To follow the rules.

Never talk back.

Do as I was fucking told.

Be the type of girl who never fought back so I could be groomed for that sonofabitch Julian to claim me.

Well, he could go to hell. The best thing I ever did was lose my virginity to Keon before Julian touched me. I reveled in knowing it was killing him that I didn't bend over so easily. And in some bizarre fated coincidence, crossing paths with Keon in the penitentiary after our time at the bar had given me an ally...or someone to look out for me. With everything going on, there was peace of mind in knowing he was there for me.

A pulse thrummed at the base of my spine when I thought of our time together yesterday, and the things he did to me. Who would have thought that being in prison would come with me finding men that brought me the most amazing orgasms? I refused to ponder how a relationship in here could actually work, because right now, he offered me an escape from the horrors within these walls.

I glanced at the round clock on the wall. Twenty to seven.

The officers walked the hallways. Prisoners snored in nearby cells. And the humming sound of the air conditioner fans continued.

As much as I loathed this place, there was a level of peacefulness when silence cloaked the building.

I pushed myself out of bed and stumbled to the sink to wash myself and get ready for my morning shift of delivering food.

Dressed, hair combed off my face, and feeling semi-normal, I flopped down on my bed and put on my black shoes, lacing them up just as the click of metal drew my attention to the door. A guard pushed it open and stood there as he did every morning when he collected me for my shift. The other cells remained locked at this time of the day and would automatically open at eight a.m.

I offered the guard a curt smile as I walked out of my cell.

He sneered at me, the healed cut across his chin deepening. "Too early to be smiling." Locking the door behind us, he turned and waved for me to follow him. We hurried toward the kitchen, and only our echoing footfalls kept us company.

Boris greeted us in the cafeteria. He was the head chef, a burly man in a deep blue apron, his long hair pulled into a ponytail. His head propped up, our gazes meeting. "Good, you're here. Selena, we are changing your shift."

"Okay, no problem."

I walked up to him as several of the other kitchen workers crossed the room to the back of the cafeteria.

"You are now to take specific deliveries to selected prisoners," he explained.

I blinked at him, unsure what he was talking about. "Like special meals?"

He huffed with pure frustration that I didn't comprehend his cryptic explanation in the first place.

"Your role is much more than just meals now, girl. Are you even listening to me?"

I bit back the words that he said no such thing, but I just stared at him, waiting for the details so I piece together this train wreck of a conversation.

"When a prisoner has specific requirements, you will be called to deliver them. And your first delivery is this morning." He glanced over to a trolley with a fresh towel, a folded prison uniform, and a white tube with no description.

My world froze, and a sour truth slid down my throat that the warden had reneged on his offer for me to work in the kitchen in exchange for Seth's crystal.

The longer I stared at the trolley, the more I pictured myself pushing that thing into cells in order to sleep with complete strangers as my duty.

Hell no!

I backed away from Boris, my heart rattling inside my rib cage, and a sickness rose to the back of my throat.

"I-I c-can't do this," I stammered.

Boris arched a brow, staring at me like I might be

mad. "You can't deliver food and fresh clothes to an inmate?"

It took moments for his words to roll over my mind. "What's in the tube?"

He glanced over to the trolley with the goods and back at me, pausing a bit too long. One corner of his mouth peeled upward. He burst into laughter, clear he'd worked out what I had been thinking.

"As far as I know, the warden's instructions were simply for you to make specific deliveries every day to whomever he requested. And that includes feeding them, washing them, keeping them company. The sex part I can't comment on, but to put you at ease, that tube is disinfectant."

I suddenly felt stupid for jumping to such a conclusion, but considering everything, it was definitely warranted.

"Now, do you think you can handle that? Your visit today is to the fae in cell 372."

"Seth." The word dribbled past my lips, and now it all made sense. The warden had just offered me every chance to spend more time with him and collect insider information from the fae. The disinfectant would come in handy. Though it felt stupid to patch him up only for the guards to punish him every day and reopen wounds.

Boris turned and marched toward the kitchen before tossing over his shoulder, "You will report here every morning for your next delivery assignment."

I nodded, even if he hadn't looked back, and I

wandered over to the trolley, deciding I ought to get this over with. The guard from this morning stood at the door, seeming to wait for me.

I marched out of the cafeteria with the trolley, the guard taking the lead, and part of me wished it had been Keon who collected me this morning.

"Selena," a female called from behind me, and I paused as one of the new kitchen hands, Elika, rushed over, carrying a tray with a large bowl, slices of bread, and utensils. The soup sloshed around the edges of the bowl, some of it splashing onto the tray, making a mess. She slid the whole thing onto the bottom shelf of the trolley and breathed heavy, staring at me with a scolding expression.

She was slightly shorter than me, thinner, and of Scandinavian descent by her features and white blonde hair.

"Boris would have murdered me if you left without the soup. Shit, Selena, next time, have some consideration for others."

"Pardon me?" I stiffened at her gruffy demeanor.

"You heard me." She lifted her chin and spun on her heels before marching back into the cafeteria. Okay, someone's an utter bitch this morning.

I ground my back teeth, because it was too freaking early to deal with people's issues.

"Don't pay her any attention," the guard explained. "She's just pissy because Boris dumped her for a younger model. Elika will sleep with anyone I hear, but then, most girls do in this joint." He snorted a laugh, and I wanted to kick him in the back of the knees so he fell flat on his face.

Not saying Elika's behavior was excusable, but no one wanted to be dumped and rejected. Hell, wars had been started by rejected lovers. And his comment about females annoyed the hell out of me.

"What about you?" he asked, and I glared at him, to which he didn't seem to notice. "You found yourself a protector in here? Every girl has one. And if you're looking for one, hit me up. Of course, there'll be a payment required." His leering gaze turned to me that time and dragged down my body.

I instantly felt dirty and sickened. A shiver ran up my spine, and I ripped my gaze from his. "I don't need your help," I hissed, both disgusted and angry that this was how this loser saw women. Assholes like him must prey on newcomers to the prison.

"If you change your mind," he continued, but I no longer listened, and instead, paid attention to the voices of the prisoners waking up.

When we paused in front of Seth's cell, the guard stood in front of the door, staring at me like he'd asked me a question. On the inside, I screamed for him to get out of my face, but I said nothing.

He tapped his name badge above his chest. Trevor. "Remember me, okay, sweets?"

I exhaled loudly, and when he finally got the message, he turned and opened the cell door. "I'll come and collect you in an hour."

I pushed the trolley inside, and I already felt the unease in my gut after my last encounter with Seth.

Thump.

I flinched and looked over my shoulder to where Trevor had locked me in here, then the asshole walked away. Great. My safety was of no concern clearly.

Across the room, the fae sat on the edge of his bed, leaning forward, elbows on his thighs, head hanging low.

My feet stopped moving, and for those few seconds, I was uncertain on the best way to approach this. In the end, I opted to keep the trolley between us until I could gauge his mood. Though in truth, I'd only ever seen him two ways... Furious, or in agonizing pain.

And neither was preferable.

The wheels of the trolley decided to squeak when I pushed it across the room, causing Seth to lift his head in my direction. He wore orange pants and a black tee stained with patches of blood. Shadows danced under his eyes, and his lips were pale. Underneath the dirt and agony lay an incredibly handsome man. Of course, those weren't the thoughts I should have when in reality, I was in danger if he decided to take out his anger on me.

"Feeling guilty again?" he asked without a thread of humor in his voice.

I licked my lips nervously and paused a few feet away. "I think the warden has taken pity on you since I'm here to bring you some food and tend to your wounds."

His light blue eyes narrowed, and yeah, I wouldn't buy that lie either, so I added, "Maybe the man has a conscience after all." I gave him a crooked grin, which he didn't react to.

"The warden is a self-serving fuckwit who will do anything for money or ancient artifacts. Everyone knows the man is easily swayed. Except calling him a man is an insult to humans."

I blinked at Seth, because that was probably the longest conversation we'd held without him wanting to toss me out of his way or throttle me. I'd take that as progress.

"Do you know what he is?" I leaned down and collected the tray of soup and placed it on the small bedside table.

When Seth didn't respond, I stood and noticed he was on his feet. He towered over me, standing proud, shoulders wide. This insanely handsome fae didn't belong in this shithole, but in a kingdom with a crown. The aura pouring from him screamed royalty, despite the stained clothes, the wounds covering his skin, and the exhaustion in his eyes. Guilt slammed through my mind that I added to his grief.

"I can do the rest myself," he demanded.

I looked over to the shut door and back at him. "I'm stuck here until they deem it has been sufficient time. So how about I apply some of the disinfectant to the wounds on your back where you can't reach?"

He shook his head and walked over to the prison door, banging his fist on it. "Guards," he bellowed.

I gritted my teeth so hard, it sent a shooting pain up into my head.

After he kept banging, he caught the attention of a guard. "Get her out of my cell now. I want her out," he growled.

I couldn't help but feel hurt that he wanted me to leave so quickly, but I said nothing when the guard looked over to me. He then proceeded to tap the piece in his ear and turned away as he murmured to security or who knows. Moments later, he opened the door, and Seth stepped aside for me to leave.

I straightened my posture, hating the embarrassed blush hitting my cheeks at the way he treated me.

Hastily, I placed the clean clothes, towel and tube on his bed, then pushed the empty trolley out of the prison. He didn't even look at me, and my stomach rolled.

Fuck. How the hell was I supposed to get close to him if he couldn't stand the sight of me?

The door shut behind me, and I didn't even look back, but marched out of there as fast as I could. Back in the kitchen, there was no sign of Boris, so I returned the trolley out the back with the others and headed into the kitchen to see if they needed help. I had to do something to keep distracted and from overthinking about how I would deal with Seth and the warden.

Days passed by.

Each morning, I'd be given a trolley with clothes, food, medicine, and even snacks for Seth. He waited for me near the door of his cell, took the goods and told the guard I couldn't stay. I would be in too much danger if I remained. So the guard removed me.

Today, I was seething that he continued to play this game, and I was going to stay in his room regardless of what he said. I had it all planned out in my head for when he addressed the guard.

I pushed the trolley, a smug smile tugging at my lips as we approached his cell. The guard opened the door, and I squared my shoulders, stepping into Seth's room.

My gaze swept to where he'd been standing the last few days, except he wasn't there. I slipped deeper into the room and found him lying in bed. My pulse thudded in my throat because it meant his last beating would have been more than severe.

The door shut with a final thud, and I moved toward his bed to find him on his stomach, his eyes barely open. I looked at his back and gasped, my stomach falling through me.

His back was a cross-cross myriad of cuts, some still open and bleeding.

My eyes pricked at seeing the cruelty, and I wanted to cry for him. I had no idea if the rumors about him killing his father were true, but I was convinced in my heart they weren't. And all I could think about was that he suffered so much.

"Selena." My name fell off his lips in a whisper.

"I'm here." I didn't waste a single moment, and I turned to the trolley where I grabbed the towel and antiseptic tube. There were also bandages in this one, and now I understood why they added them in the trolley. Part of me felt sick to my stomach to think the warden had Seth beaten this morning so terribly to stop him from throwing me out of his cell.

I shook with anger at the warden, and I wanted him to hurt and feel this pain. In haste, I collected the empty bowl of food on his bedside table and filled it with water. Then I dragged the small stool and sat near him with the strip of bandages and tape in my lap.

"I-I'm alright," he groaned, barely able to speak.

"Sure you are." I wet one end of the towel lightly and lightly patted his pack.

He arched slightly, hissing.

"I promise I will be quick, but this will stop an infection." I didn't stop wiping the wounds until most of the blood was gone.

"Fae heal fast," he muttered, like somehow that alleviated the agony he was going through.

Unscrewing the lid from the disinfectant, I answered, "Does that mean your injuries won't get infected, because I somehow doubt that."

He twisted his head to look up at me, his lips tightening. "What do you know about fae that makes you so sure of yourself?"

I tossed my head back and shrugged, then squeezed out a long line of cream onto my finger. "I know fae are arrogant and stubborn. They would rather suffer in silence than even admit they need help."

A growl hummed deep in his throat. "And what about you, siren-girl? Pushy. Must have the last word. I'm guessing very disobedient, and atrocious at lying."

"I. Am. Not. Any of those things," I snapped, and lathered the cream over his wounds, maybe a bit too harshly.

Seth groaned, his whole body stiffening from the sting. "And you like to inflict pain."

"Yep, you finally got one thing right," I confessed and eased off the pressure.

His eyes shut, the muscles in his arms tensing as I finished applying the antiseptic.

The cream had blended with some of the blood, turning into a pinkish hue, but I didn't stop until I covered every cut. Gingerly, I ran my finger outside the edges of the wounds I could only imagine were done by a whip.

When I wiped my hand on the towel, Seth opened his eyes and looked at me, something new flaring over his mesmerizing eyes. They gleamed.

"What has the warden promised you?" he asked.

"Huh?"

"Be a good girl and open your eyes to when you're being used."

My hands fisted the towel in my lap, and I imagined myself charging out of there...but that was exactly what he wanted. And I wouldn't let him win. "You are rude and insufferable. You don't even know me to say that shit. You have no idea what I've gone through or am going through. And you know what? When I was asked to help you, I jumped at the idea because I felt bad for giving away your crystal. So if that makes me a terrible

person, then hell, I must be the worst in this penitentiary."

Sure, I exaggerated…a lot…but he had me fuming.

"Then tell me? About yourself," he asked.

Never, was my initial thought, then it occurred to
me this might be his way of reaching out to me.

I ripped off a piece of bandage and tape and started
plastering his back. "I'm an ordinary girl who grew up
in an over-protective family and was being groomed
for a horrible life, then I ended up in this joint."

Seth laughed, then broke into painful groans, his
eyes squinting shut.

I wanted to say, served you right, but I couldn't
bring myself to do so when he suffered so much. And
this was why I wasn't made for a life in prison.

When he finally quieted down, he murmured, "You
are anything but ordinary."

A sudden blush of heat hit my cheeks, convinced he
just gave me a compliment. Maybe. I didn't really
know.

But I focused on his back, running my index finger
over the edges of the tape holding down his bandages,
at the flow of muscles over his torso beneath the patch-
work of injuries. He was definitely a work of art, and I
traced the tips of my fingers over the softness of his
skin between the dressing. I followed the curves, liking
how he felt under my touch.

"Listen, Seth," I started. "You may hate me, but we
need to work together. I think the warden is punishing
you for not letting me stay in your cell to help you out."

His brows pinched together. "Why does he want you here with me?" he groaned.

The response tittered on the edge of my mind, but I couldn't bring myself to tell him. He'd never open up to me if he knew I had so much to lose as well. Telling Seth the truth wouldn't do me any favors.

"He's a bastard," I answered. "You think he wants anyone to go against his order? He's flexing his power, that's all. So stop telling the guard to get rid of me. Please. I'll sit in a corner and read or something, but I can't see you like this." My breath caught in my chest, and I swallowed hard.

For a long moment, I kept tracing his back, which seemed to calm him down.

When there was no response, and I glanced down, he breathed heavily, his eyes shut and asleep. My presence alone calmed people, and combined with my soothing touch, it definitely helped put him at ease. But had he heard my warning?

Slowly, I got him from the chair and packed up everything on the trolley when white chalk lines drew my attention underneath the dressing table near the bed.

I blinked, curious to what it could be, so I shifted the small piece of furniture aside and stared down to the dark stone ground. And looking back at me was a beautiful sketch of me. I could barely breathe. Seth drew an image of me.

Long hair flowed over my shoulders as if caught in a wind, my eyes were huge and glimmered, my lips slightly parted. The expression he captured was that of sorrow...a girl lost in a dark world. Was that how he saw me?

Groaning, he slowly shifted in the bed.

I frantically replaced the small table over the drawing, still unable to believe he thought of me to the point that he'd illustrate me. And he was talented.

A shadow fell over me from the door, and I looked over to find the guard. Had it really been an hour?

Taking the trolley, I pushed it across the room as the guard unlocked the door.

I took one last glance over my shoulder to Seth, who hadn't stirred. Then my attention dipped to the bedside table and the few lines of white chalk sticking out. Why was he sketching me?

CHAPTER 5

SELENA

The next day when I reached Seth's room, he slouched on his bed, wearing only orange uniform pants, the bandages on his back still present from yesterday. Warmth flooded me that perhaps the warden pulled back on the daily punishment while I cared for him.

"Did you sleep well?" I asked.

His eyes seemed paler today when he met my gaze, like the clearest ocean waters, revealing everything beneath the surface. If I looked into them too long, it felt like I might fall into them and never find my way out.

My pulse suddenly beat too fast, too hard, and I lowered my eyes, noting the white chalk lines under the bedside table were gone, and only dusty remnants remained. Had he seen me looking at it the day before?

"Cat got your tongue?" I teased when he gave no reply. Instead he grinned.

I pushed the trolley right in front of his bed, which carried a plastic bucket with soapy warm water and face towels and more dry ones.

"You going to just sit there and smirk?" I continued as I eyed his broad, strong shoulders, every solid muscle, the narrowing of his waist, and the thin line of blond hair funneling down the middle of his stomach and disappearing beneath his pants.

He shook his head, then he returned to being silent, and I wondered how much of him was broken. Was his aloofness a game fae played, or his way of dealing with my company after being beaten day in and day out for gods knew how long?

I reached into the bucket and pulled out a face towel and wrung the water out of it, then turned to him, taking a seat on the small stool. It brought me to his eye level.

Uncertainty coiled in my chest, as I couldn't read his expression. So instead, I ran the wet fabric over his collarbone where something black stained his skin.

His nostrils flared, and he took a deep breath.

"Does it hurt?" I asked.

"It's hot."

I gave him a few moments, then continued washing him. His hair hung loosely around his face as messily as I remembered, the tiredness from his eyes faded, and the earlier scratch on his shoulder from yesterday seemed to be completely healed over. He wasn't wrong when he told me fae healed quickly.

Carefully, I wiped over his chest, his muscles, his arms.

Something warm sparked alight in my gut and came to life the longer I studied his perfect body and touched him.

He didn't move, but sat back, watching me drag the wet face towel across his stomach. I felt his eyes on me intensifying. And when I glanced up, we got lost in each other's eyes, like we'd forgotten where we were. Like a carved sliver of time revealing how much more could be possible if we were anywhere but in Nightmare Penitentiary.

What would he taste like if we kissed? Like salvation or the sweetest treat? It was such a ridiculous thought to have about a fae who was on death row, that much was obvious. With a fae who barely spoke to me and would do anything to get me out of his face.

I returned the towel to the water, washed it quickly, and rinsed the water before swiveling back toward Seth.

My gaze settled on the erection tenting his pants, and it took me several moments to decide I ought to stop staring. That window of pretending I never saw it has long sailed away when I meet his stretching grin. I rolled my eyes at him, even if my first reaction was to reach down and palm his cock to discover if he was as thick and big as he looked.

This wasn't what I expected from the fae who'd been ignoring me for days, who growled at almost everything I said. And now… Something tangled in the pit of my gut to see how my touch affected him.

I'd fallen victim to Alaric and Keon already. Though 'victim' was very much the wrong word, since I craved and wanted them just as much as they did me. But in truth, Seth physically shouldn't surprise me. He'd been tortured for so long, most likely having no other company, so a female's touch would definitely entice desires.

Honestly, I had no clue on how I should respond.

I pulled back and took the towel to wipe my hands while my face burned. I licked my lips and chewed on the lower one as I tried to get over acting like a shy school kid.

I'd have liked to think I could hold myself back when it came to such handsome men and their arousal, especially as my experience had been very limited to men from this penitentiary.

"Does my cock embarrass you?" he asked casually, when for the longest time, I remained with my back to him, my cheeks on fire.

I turned around to see him leaning back on his hands on the bed, making no effort to conceal his growing arousal. He seriously was getting off on seeing me squirm. "What are you talking about? I don't see anything out of the ordinary." I smirked at him, and he laughed, then reached down and groped himself over his pants as if to prove his point.

"Maybe next time, I'll ask the warden to give me something for itchiness if you're having trouble down there." I arched a brow in his direction, but he was on his feet so fast, my heart slammed into my throat.

A shiver slinked up my spine, and heat pooled between my thighs instantly, like his presence flipped on a switch inside me. I had a horny switch apparently, because suddenly, I struggled to breathe.

When had it gotten so hot in the cell?

"If you're having trouble, I can help you? Would you like that?" he stated, as if he could read my feelings all over my face. I wouldn't be surprised, as I was terrible at hiding how I felt. And this was why I could never play poker, as I'd give everything away in two seconds.

I looked up into his alluring blue eyes, feeling like what was intensifying between us was inevitable. Like a brewing storm, the emotions I started to feel for Seth grew, and trying to stop them was impossible. They would strike, whether I liked them or not. My chest tightened, knowing I was right.

I hated myself for it.

Loathed my body for responding so irrationally.

For feeling so out of control.

Which seemed to have been the story of my life, and also how I ended up in this awful place. Where the universe never dealt me easy cards, now did it? Me melting in the presence of such powerful men was definitely my weakness.

God, how could I be attracted so strongly to three men at once?

Seth reached over, his fingers gripping my chin and

forcing me to look up at me. "You never answered my question, siren-girl."

For the life of me, I couldn't remember what he'd asked, not when my heart was racing and my insides resembled lava from an exploding volcano. I wasn't thinking of anything else but how I turned into a mess so quickly.

His grip didn't waiver, and I couldn't stop staring at his full lips, thinking about what it would be like to kiss a fae. My breaths wedged in my lungs, and I might have lost my mind at how easily a single touch from him swayed me.

The metallic clang of metal drew my attention to the opening door of the cell.

A guard stepped inside, and I wasn't sure if I was relieved or disappointed about the interruption. My heart felt like the ball from the ping pong game the inmates had been playing in the communal area, swinging back and forth between my torn emotions.

Two more guards entered the cell, and the room suddenly felt constricting. "It's time," the main guard with a hooked nose announced, his gaze locked on Seth, not me.

My stomach dropped, because I knew exactly where they were taking Seth. And I wanted to cry, but instead, I pushed myself between them and the fae. "Have mercy, please. Give him a day of no torture."

The guard rolled his eyes at me. "Get the hell out of my way."

I stood my ground, well aware my small protest

would achieve little, but if I did nothing, I would feel even more guilty about what Seth was going through.

"Your lover boy is safe for now, unless you consider taking him to the psychiatrist punishment, then move," he barked in my face.

His words fell into my place in my mind, and while part of me felt silly, I moved out of his way.

Seth strolled past me toward the guards, his gaze on mine. "It almost sounds like you care about me." The guards grabbed his arm and wrenched him out of the cell.

I stood alone in the room for a few moments, trying to piece together how quickly the tables had turned. But maybe this was a good thing and would mean next time, he'd be more open to talking about his past.

Once they all left, I pushed the trolley out of there. I sure as hell hadn't planned for that to happen. Instead of getting any information from him, I ended up getting aroused and stumbling over my breaths.

What in the world just happened?

By the time I'd returned the trolley to the kitchen, cleaned up, and had something to eat, I still couldn't stop thinking about Seth.

An hour later, I paced in my cell from the back wall to the entrance, thinking about how I felt around Seth, his damn erection, and even the image he had drawn of me on the ground.

He was an artist, and I wanted to give him something that he could use as an escape from the beatings. A drawing pad, pencils, maybe colored chalk. I didn't know, but the more I thought about it, the more the idea grew on me. And from what I'd seen so far in this place, if there was someone who might be able to assist me in getting things, it would be either Keon or Alaric. So I'd start with Keon first, as I figured he might be more open to helping.

Outside my cell, a few inmates hung around, chatting. Guards were posted at most corners, watching everything. I swung in the direction of Trevor, the guard who took me to Seth's cell most mornings.

He grinned at my approach, and while my skin crawled at the sight, I offered him a tight smile as well.

"I know somewhere we can go," he offered eagerly, his gaze shifting to the empty hallway behind him. I held back the gagging reflex hitting the back of my throat. It wasn't that the man wasn't handsome. He was average build, average looking, average personality. I tried my hardest not to collect men during my time in this place, and for him, I felt nothing.

I shook my head. "Do you know where I can find Keon?"

He physically stiffened, his shoulders rising, as if just the name of his colleague sent him into an angry frenzy. "You be careful around him, understand? He has a dark side." And as if a light had been switched on, the concerned expression faded to one of joy.

Hmm, perhaps it was Dr. Jekyll and Mr. Hyde I should be cautious of. I lifted my chin and asked again, "Do you know where Keon is?"

"Not his shift yet." His response came back clipped

and fast. Then he marched away, groaning under his breath.

Alright, well then, I guessed I was paying Alaric a visit.

I sucked in a deep breath and headed down the hallway that led to the area where the seedier inmates were placed. But all I intended to do was walk through those corridors fast, and if I found no signs of him, then I was out of there. There were enough guards to keep me safe.

Ignoring the niggling worry at the back of my mind, I kept going. Nightmare Penitentiary was enormous, and it felt like I'd walked for miles when it couldn't have been more than fifty yards.

Head low.

No eye contact.

I avoided the shadowy corridors, or getting too close to the inmates in locked cells. Soon enough, the walls changed from a pasty white to deep gray, stealing the faint light overhead. Too many shadows, despite the lofty ceiling. I cranked my head up to the next level up of railings with metal wire, so no one up there could throw others over to fall to their deaths. Voices hummed like cicadas, loud and constant. Eyes were on me, I felt them heavily, and the walls seemed to be closing in around me.

Moving faster, I scanned the block numbers next to each cell, searching for Alaric's, when I paused on 666. Inside that prison, stood a young girl, maybe my age. She was thin with bright blue hair and hanging off the barred door like it was a dancing pole. She met my gaze and winked before sticking her forked tongue out. A skin-toned tail whipped out from behind her and coiled around a bar. When her eyes glinted, I knew exactly what she was. A demon.

When those things come into the human realm to steal souls, they get punished like the rest of us and end up in this nightmare.

Footfalls closed in behind me all of a sudden, a shadow cloaking me.

I quickened my pace, my heart racing.

Someone screamed up ahead, and I glanced up to spot a centaur charging down the hall in my direction. Everyone threw themselves out of his way.

His nostrils flared as his hooves thundered against the stone floor. He stood so tall, grinning and loving how everyone got out of his way. His bottom half was a deep chestnut color, and I might've been captivated to stare at such a creature. But not when it was about to mow me down.

I hurled myself toward the wall to get out of the madman's way.

Strong hands clasped around my waist. "Got you."

I flinched around and shoved my hands into the chest out of instinct of the man before me. His eyes were vertical slits like a snake's and a copper color, just like the few scales running across his temples.

Snake charmer. These shifters took serpent form and venom ran in their veins. They were known for being territorial, and their favorite kind of girls were rodent shifters. Could they be any more cliché?

A shiver curled up over my spine as I pushed away from him.

"Been watching you." He stepped closer, his tongue slipping out and sweeping over his upper lip. "You came here with such purpose." His hand lashed out, grabbing my neck, and pulled me toward him. "Who has attracted the attention of a siren, that she comes to them with determination? I always thought it was the other way around and everyone came when the siren called." The corners of his mouth curled upward, a small dimple appearing in his wide chin. It matched his broad forehead, and overall, he just had a square head. He stood taller than me, like most men seemed to do, his chest rising and falling quickly, like he expected me to run so he could hunt me down. The predatory hunger behind those snake-eyes terrified me.

"Leave me alone. I'm not interested."

His hand threaded through my hair and fisted it, wrenching me toward him so our faces were inches apart. His breaths stunk of death, but I refused to show him my fear.

That made me weak and easier prey.

I shoved my hand into his chest once again, harder this time, and ripped free of his grip. "I said fuck off. I'm not here for you and have business with someone you don't want to deal with. Trust me."

He cocked his head to the side, eyeing me up and down, leaving me feeling filthy, but I stood tall regardless. "I like fucking feisty women. It's even better when they act like they don't want it."

A small crowd had gathered around us now, and unease flared over me, as I frantically scanned the area for the quickest way to make a run for it out of here. Why did I think it was smart to come into this sector anyway?

"Whoever you came to visit can wait," he hissed, and snatched my arm and hauled me with him away from the crowd.

I screamed out of pure instinct, and shoved my free fist into his arm, but it made no impact, not with this fiend.

"Get the fuck away from me." I kicked him in the leg hard enough that he swung me around to face him.

"Your choice, dollface. Here or in my cell, I don't give a shit, but I'm fucking you today."

Fear spiked through me. "You'll regret ever touching me."

He barked a laugh in my face. "I'll regret not taking you right now against the wall."

I hated how he looked at me as though I was nothing but a means to pleasure. I tugged against him when someone threw themselves at Snake-Eyes, coming from somewhere behind us.

He was ripped away from me, and I stumbled forward from the momentum.

It took me moments to realize that Alaric straddled Snake-Eyes, laying punch after punch into his face so aggressively, I couldn't help but cheer on the inside. I hated violence, but seeing him fight on my behalf sent excitement to the pit of my gut with that whole protector vibe he had going.

Three others jumped on Alaric's back and wrenched him off the asshole.

I looked to the end of the hall, where a guard strolled past. He glanced this way but kept on walking, and my insides clenched. That was when I looked around and found no cameras in the corners. This was a black spot, and the security in this place knew it but did nothing.

Alaric was at my side, his gaze wild with fury, his mouth twisted, and he was fuming. "Why are you here?" He clasped my waist and plastered me to his side like he owned me, and I stuck to him, because he was exactly where I wanted to be.

Snake-Eyes shoved forward, licking the blood at the corner of his mouth and glaring at me, then at Alaric.

"She's mine," the serpent dick spat the words, half a dozen goons behind him. "You know the rules, Alaric. What you find out here, you keep. You agreed to that rule."

Alaric straightened, his chin high, and there wasn't a sliver of concern from him. But his hand tightening around my waist told a different tale. He was worried about me. And hell, so was I. If I had known such factions existed, I never would have come to find Alaric. I'd have sent a message or something to get him to see me.

"Not this time," Alaric growls. "I've claimed her long

before this, and she's my property. You touch, and I'll rip that fucking lizard dick right off."

Snake-Eyes' upper lip curled upward, twisting into hatred. Part of me prayed he was smart enough to walk away, but that was a joke. A group of alphas, filled on testosterone, weren't going anywhere.

These kinds of men wouldn't back down.

"Then we fight for her," Snake-Eyes declared. "Winner keeps her for good."

My heart pounded in my chest.

"Agreed," Alaric stated too damn fast.

Panic collided into me, and I turned to him. "Wait what? You're going to gamble on me?"

"Honey cheeks, you having doubts about me?" He stared at me with such a sexy expression, like I had nothing in the world to worry about.

I scanned the gang Snake-Eyes had with him, half a dozen of them, and then I looked back to my gorgeous incubus. God, he was so huge and strong, and the way he attacked that bastard in the first placed hummed inside me. But we were outnumbered if they decided to all turn on us.

"Fuck yeah. I believe in you," I stated.

"Let's get this shitshow started," Snake-Eyes shouted.

And before I knew it, we were all marching deeper into the hallway, and then several turns later, we emerged into an open courtyard. I hadn't seen this section before. It was the size of a basketball court, enclosed by lofty metal fences with barbed wire across the top.

Beyond the fence were stone walls, and they reminded me of the first time I arrived at the penitentiary. When we walked through the front gates, the stone walls closed in around me. And here they were, bringing back so many memories.

I glanced behind us, and the prison hovered over it like a giant, but there were no windows overlooking this section. These prisoners were given a small piece of outside haven, except it seemed they used it as a battle ground.

Around us, other inmates poured outside, and I felt queasy at how quickly things were getting out of control.

"Are you sure about this?" I whispered to Alaric.

He swept me up and into his arms, and instinctually, I wrapped my legs around his waist as we faced each other. He walked us onto the court while everyone else gathered around the court.

"I promise to make you a rug out of his viper skin if you ask me too, babe. Now kiss me."

My head spun with everything and how quickly we ended up in a death arena.

All I wanted was some drawing equipment for Seth, not to have Alaric pitched against a hellish snake charmer.

I kissed him, our mouths clashed, our tongues tangled in a battle of their own. The passion between us flared, and heat dove to the apex between my legs.

His hands cupped my ass, and I couldn't get enough of this huge man. He'd crawled into my veins, and now I desired him unbearably.

The crowd cheered around us, and when we broke apart, I gasped for air like my existence depended on him. What the hell had he done to me?

"Missed you the last few days," he said. "But next time you want to see me, no need to draw so much attention." He smirked at me, and I couldn't work out if I wanted to laugh or cry.

I clasped my hands on either side of his face. "Please don't die."

"I'll never let that piece of shit touch you again." He kissed me once more, then lowered me onto my feet. Next thing, two females rushed up to me, one on either side, and quickly grasped my arms.

I shuddered and terror fell through me as they roughly pinned my back to the wire fence and stretched my arms out on either side of me. "What are you doing?"

They didn't respond as the girls bound my wrists to the wire fence with rope. My heart slammed into my rib cage as I fought to pull away from them.

"Alaric?" I cried out.

CHAPTER 6

SELENA

laric watched the girls bind me to the wire fence while my breaths raced. "Babe, this is part of the fight rules in this court. You're safe for now."

"For now?" I exclaimed.

He stared at me so calmly while my pulse hammered through my veins, yet he was the one about to fight for my safety. Once I'd been tied up, he stepped closer once more, our cheeks were touching, his mouth in my ear.

"When this is over, I want you tied up and naked for me." His words coupled with that deep, husky voice undid me.

Hell, here I was, an object to be fought over in front of spectators, and yet my panties were soaking wet. I needed a major reorder of my priorities if I ever came out of this with my sanity.

Alaric swung away from me and marched into the

center of the court, while the spectators remained watching from around the edges of the arena, steering away from me.

Snake-Eyes strode forward, unbuttoning his shirt, then taking it off and tossing it aside. A huge green and black serpent tattoo covered his chest, while others coiled around his arms.

The crowd boomed with excitement, hands pumping into the air, and I could swear I'd just walked into the *Mad Max* movie. This was utter madness, yet I couldn't take my eyes off the men...more specifically, Alaric. He stood taller, broader, and I had no idea how I even gained the attention of such a man.

An older man with a shaved head and goatee stepped out of the crowds, his hands in the air before lowering them, and the crowd silenced. "Rules are easy," he explained loudly. "No killing your opponent. First person to not get up off the ground for five seconds without being held down wins the siren." He threw a glance my way, and a shiver wrapped around my chest.

My heart beat crazily, and I prayed with everything that Alaric won. He better win, as I was more fucked up than I ever thought if he didn't. And I doubted even Keon would be able to save me from this snake charmer.

The older man released a sharp, low whistle, and stepped away from the warriors.

Snake-Eyes attacked first, lunging at Alaric, who ducked and spun on his heels. Then he drove a fist to the middle of his enemy's back. The man arched but never once cried out.

Instead, he whipped around with speed and struck at Alaric. Coming at him faster and harder.

The punches flew, each taking and giving, and I was convinced just one of those hits would knock me out cold.

My heart was going to give out. They'd started their war dance.

Alaric ducked a swinging fist, throwing himself into a forward roll. But Snake-Eyes moved so freakily fast, that he lunged onto Alaric's back, an arm locked around his throat, the other fist slamming into the side of his head.

A scream escaped past my lips. I felt sick to my stomach at watching Alaric collapse to his knees.

Blowing a gasp of air through his lips, Alaric thrust his fist up and over his head, slamming it into Snake-Eyes' head, over and over. In seconds, Alaric burst free, roaring like a lion, shoving his opponent back onto his ass. Butterflies exploded through my gut at watching how powerful Alaric stood, fighting for me. As crazy as it sounded, if we had sex now, I'd be willing to have his child. The sex-induced hormones inside me were driving me insane with a desire I never expected at seeing Alaric fight.

He swung back into the fight, just as Snake-Eyes delivered a round-house kick, his heel colliding into the side of Alaric's face.

Blood sprayed outward, splattering the basketball

court. Alaric clasped his bloody mouth and wiped it clean, his expression twisting with rage, his shoulders lifting, as did his shoulder blades. He resembled a predatory wolf about to attack. "You fucking piece of shit."

Something was happening to lizard breath as his whole body trembled, and in a heartbeat, the serpent tattoo on his chest lashed out, mouth gaping open, fangs poised to bite. The thing was still attached to his body like it was him.

"Watch out," I yelled, just as Alaric threw himself backward, the fangs missing him by a sliver.

"He's cheating," I cried out.

Then the asshole turned to me, the snake sweeping in my direction, suspended outward from his chest. "Won't be long before you meet king cobra." He reached down and grabbed his groin.

I scrunched up my nose and face. "I'd rather die."

Alaric rushed at him from the side, and both of them hit the ground hard. One hand snatched the serpent just behind the head, and the other grasped the asshole's neck, pinning him to the ground.

"Don't you fucking look at her. She doesn't exist to you, or I'll rip your eyes out." Alaric's threat was a poem in my ears.

The snake struck out of his hold, and I flinched against the metal fence at my back, knocking my head a bit too hard. Alaric threw himself up and after the thing. I couldn't even look, and clamped my eyes shut as fear strangled me.

Grunts and thumping sounds intensified.

When I cracked open an eye, Alaric was down on one knee, holding back the serpent with two hands, straining, his muscles bulging. The viper's mouth stood inches from his face, while Snake-Eyes raised his fists for a final deathly hit.

In a sudden shift, Alaric bellowed with anger and drove himself to his feet, swiftly kneeing the asshole in the balls.

Everyone booed and boomed in protest.

Snake-Eyes hit the ground, grabbing himself, while his snake slithered back over his chest, flattening into a tattoo.

A sharp whistle cut through the racket, and the earlier older man stepped forward, making a T-sign with his hands to indicate break time.

Alaric stumbled backward, his energy drained. He came over to me, blood smeared across his cheek from the busted lip. My heart drummed against my rip cage at the insanity of what I'd just watched. Snake-Eyes was a dirty fighter...of course he was, but my man was a fucking powerful god, and he'd demolish him. And now he just needed an incentive to turn the odds in his favor and end this goddamn fight, because no way in hell was I going to ever let a slithering snake charmer touch me.

"He's going down," he muttered, the strikes he'd received clearly affecting his posture and endurance with the way he breathed heavily.

"Alaric," I coaxed with soft words. "I have a confession."

He stared at me with intensity and closed in, one hand propped up against the metal fence behind me, the other on my cheek. "Talk to me?" His voice was raspy and rough.

"Seeing you out there fighting is making me so fucking horny. I'm so wet for you," I gasped in his ear, sounding so stupid in my head and corny.

His hand unexpectedly went straight to my heat, fingers groping my pussy over my pants. And I flinched as that wasn't what I expected, but clearly, my corny confession lured him in.

"Fuck," he mumbled, nuzzling my neck, pushing himself up against me, practically dry humping me in front of everyone. And I melted against him, pushing myself to get closer. Something about Alaric drove me insane… Of course I knew it was related to him being an incubus, or at least I wish I could use that as an excuse since I'd been able to resist his allure.

Everything I felt here was all me.

"Go and win this, then I'm yours."

"You have no idea what you do to me." He kissed me, and I gently gnawed on his lower lip. "You're mine," he murmured, and spun back toward the arena.

The crowd burst into a cheering roar. And the two men charged at each other and slammed together in a thundering clap.

This was different to the first round, where it felt like they had tested the waters of each others' powers.

Now, they moved so fast, their actions were a blur and all I caught were snippets of arms and legs, the grunts blending in with the cheering crowd.

"Destroy him, Alaric," I yelled out as his self-appointed cheerleader. Completely selfish on my part, and because the more I watched Alaric fight for me, the more I craved him.

It happened so fast that time. Moments later, Snake-Eyes was tossed half way across the court and hit the ground so hard, I heard the snap of something in his body. I cringed as it sounded painful.

He cried out, but he was moving.

Ten.

Nine.

Eight.

The spectators were counting down with me now, loudly.

Five.

Four.

Three.

The dickhead pushed to his hands and knees, but he collapsed back down, falling face first.

One.

"Yes!" I shouted with exhilaration. Alaric won. And I wouldn't become a snake charmer's sex slave.

Everyone broke into chatter, mingling about, excited by the entertainment they'd just experienced.

Snake-Eyes groaned on the ground, trying to push himself up again, but he collapsed back down. Two of his goons swooped in and dragged him up by his arms and helped him out of the court.

The masses started leaving and heading back into the building, all talking loudly, laughing and patting each other's backs for what I could only imagine were successful bets on Alaric winning that fight.

"Angel," Alaric rasped, standing in front of me, scratched and bruised, but victorious. And just having him stand in front of me, claiming me as his prize, was enough to send ripples of arousal through my body like electric shocks.

"You're fucking incredible," I groaned, lifting my head to look up into his spectacular eyes.

He reached over to untie me from my fence, and once free, I threw myself into his arms, climbing up him like he was a damn tree. His large hands gripped my waist and lifted me with ease to reach his mouth. My legs and arms clenched around him like vines desperately needing purchase. His presence sent me straight to a world of desire.

We kissed passionately as he slammed my back against the metal fence, his erection pressing to my heat. I rocked my hips back and forth, needing the friction to satisfy the growing desire.

Then he broke from my mouth and licked my lips, making his way to my neck, his lips on my earlobe. I glanced over to the court to find we were completely alone. Just us and the concrete arena with a refreshing breeze blowing through.

He growled as his hand dipped between us and

slipped under the elastic of my prison pants and under-wear. Fingers gilded lower over my small mound of hair to where an inferno lay. Where I was spread open as I straddled his hips.

Fingers played over my inner lips. I arched in his arms, so close to exploding it took everything in me to not come so freaking fast.

He pulled at my lips, sending me into shudders. I moaned, my nipples hardening.

"You have the perfect pussy," he complimented me as he slid two fingers into me.

My head fell back against the fence, my legs trem-bling as he claimed my mouth, kissing me heavily. His fingers worked into me, and damn, he had large fingers. When he tried to press another in there, I tensed.

"Let me in, angel. I promise you'll enjoy it."

I was too far gone to fight against being turned on. I eased and let him have me any which way, and shifted to offer him easier access.

Slowly, he pushed another finger into me, and it slid in easier once he had the tip in. The arousal and pain of being stretched came at me.

"I want my mouth and tongue on that sweet tight hole."

One second, I was moaning, the next, an orgasm slammed into me, ripping through me.

He swallowed my screams, not releasing me, continuing to finger me, kissing me as I convulsed beneath him with the most incredible climax. Dutifully, he never stopped pleasuring me until I floated from my arousal.

"Sweet Jesus," I murmured, breathing hard.

"This area is out of bounds," a male's voice boomed, stealing the perfect moment where I was losing myself to Alaric, where I needed him to fuck me.

He deftly removed his fingers from inside me and out of my pants, then lowered me to my feet.

"Alaric, the warden wants to see you."

"Fuck!" he looked over to me. "Come, walk with us as it will get you out of this sector safely." We started walking toward the guards when he looked over and asked, "I'm curious. Why did you come and see me today?"

"It's stupid and none of this stuff was meant to happen, but I wanted to ask if you could get me a sketch set for drawing."

He blinked at me as though just realizing he'd just battled a snake charmer and risked his life for drawing equipment.

I wanted to laugh at it myself when I considered what we went through, but I somehow doubted he'd find it funny. And I sure as hell wasn't telling him it was for Seth and not me.

CHAPTER 7

SELENA

I lay in my bed, absentmindedly watching water drip from the ceiling at the foot of my bed. The drip was new. I had long since given up on trying to keep anything in my cell dry. As soon as I would find a way to stop one drip, another one would start somewhere even more annoying. It was like my cell was cursed to annoy me.

On second thought, it probably was cursed to do that. I would have to see what Keon knew about that.

Keon... Just the thought of him made me smile. We were walking a dangerous line. What we were doing put both of us at risk. I had a feeling that the warden knew much of what happened in the prison and that he let certain things slide up to a certain point. It was just a matter of time before Keon and I were used against each other.

But I couldn't imagine giving him up.

Alaric's face appeared in my mind next. My body

clenched just thinking of him. His fight with that snake charmer asshole who attacked me had gone a long way in softening my heart towards him. Not to mention the way his body had looked as he faced his prey, how he took up the challenge to protect me without hesitation. And then our kiss afterward sent tingles to the pit of my stomach. That man melted me on the spot.

I called Snake-Eyes prey because there was no way to miss the fact that Alaric was a predator.

"Squeak, squeak."

I sat up in bed and eagerly looked towards the hole in the corner of my cell.

My little friend came scurrying out, dragging what looked like a scroll. I got off my cot and knelt down on the ground so that he could hop into my hand. It was amazing how he could haul things that were three, four times his bodyweight.

"What do you have for me today?" I asked, stroking his back softly. The mouse preened under my attention, flopping in my hand to showcase his belly. I obliged him, and I swore that he purred under my touch.

When I'd finally given him the attention he was looking for, he nosed the rolled piece of paper towards me.

I unrolled it quizzically. My heart began to hammer as soon as I started to read. It was an invite to a dinner...from Alaric. Just the sight of his name made my body heat up. A dinner invitation, not something I had expected in a place like this. In a way, I almost had more freedom here than I had in my life before this. Any dinner invitations I was accepting prior to Nightmare Penitentiary consisted of dinners that had been carefully vetted by my mother and Julian. They served a specific purpose, whether it was to charm a business associate of Julian, or just to serve as arm candy to whatever vampire had been sent by Julian that day. Once I turned eighteen, those business dinners would have evolved…into more extracurricular activities for those clients.

I shivered at the thought and quickly pushed it away. I wasn't going back to that life. It wasn't happening.

A tiny squeak brought my attention back to the present, and I examined the note once again. It didn't give any specific directions for how I was to attend this dinner party. I looked at the ugly prison outfit I was wearing and sighed. Definitely not like the other dinner parties, where I had been dressed in whatever designer dress Julian wanted to see me in that day or that I scrounged from my mother's luxe closet.

At the bottom of the invitation, Alaric had drawn two boxes. In a surprisingly elegant script, he had written 'yes' and 'no' under the boxes. I giggled at the thought of big bad Alaric putting something so elementary in a dinner invitation, and it made me want to attend even more. I didn't have a pen, so I took a rock from the ground and made a sharp slice in the 'yes' box. I then rolled the document into a scroll and gave it to the little mouse who squeaked…almost excitedly. Maybe my little friend had an interest in my love life.

I snorted at the thought. Prior to this place, I'd never imagined that my best friend would be a mouse. Maybe I was going crazy after all.

The mouse scurried away, and I laid back on my lumpy cot, staring again at the drips falling from my ceiling.

I must have dozed off, because the clang of my cell opening startled me. I sat up blearily, looking to see who it was. While I did have some freedom here, there was a usual schedule to the day. The last surprise visit I'd had on the day of my mother's visit had not been a good one, and I wasn't looking forward to a repeat.

A guard I'd never seen before strode in with a familiar silver box. He sat it down at the foot of my cot without looking at me and quickly left without a glance back. The sound of the door closing settled my nerves.

Puzzled, I looked at the box, wondering why there would be a high-end department store box on my bed...or even in the prison at all.

Alaric. It must be from him. Hadn't that been the reason I went to see him about the sketch kit I wanted for Seth, because he was known to be able to get anything he wanted around the prison? Feeling a flicker of excitement I hadn't experienced in a while, I ripped open the box and stared a little dazed at the silver slip of fabric I held in my hands. It didn't look big enough to cover my left butt cheek let alone my entire body.

The way that the dress was somehow sparkling in the dim lighting in the cell convinced me to try it on… just to see.

I stood in the corner, where someone was least likely to see me, and slipped off my uniform. With almost reverence, because the beautiful dress didn't seem to belong in such a filthy place as my cell, I slipped the dress over my head. After the rough fabric of my prison suit, it felt a little bit like I was slipping on a piece of heaven. I smoothed the fabric down over my thighs.

I was right. The dress didn't cover a lot. But it did cover enough. It was relatively modest looking at it from the front I was sure. Besides the fact that it was obscenely short, the top of the dress was high, showing no hint of cleavage. It was the back that would really get you. Feeling around with my hands, I could tell that the dress was open all the way down to right above my ass. It definitely wasn't a dress I could wear a bra with, so I slipped off the bra I had been wearing.

I didn't know how I felt about walking through the halls of this place in this dress. I'm sure that would make the threats from the other prisoners even worse.

At that thought, my cell door suddenly clanged open again. Another guard I hadn't seen before stepped in carrying a tan shoe box embossed with the Christian Louboutin insignia.

My heart skipped a few beats. My mother had never

let me borrow her pairs of Louboutins, and Julian had been more partial to whatever shoes looked most like stripper shoes.

The guard once again set down the box and left without looking at me once. I wondered again at the power Alaric had in this place...and why he wasn't using it to get out of here. The guard didn't even give one glance at my dress, despite the fact that it was sparkly enough to outshine a disco ball.

I walked over to the shoe box and tentatively opened the lid, gasping when I saw a pair of metallic silver sandals with the familiar red bottoms. I squealed a little loudly in excitement and was quickly sobered when someone a few cells down yelled for me to "shut the hell up."

Frowning, I slipped on the shoes, and this time, withheld my squeal at the fact that they fit perfectly. I wasn't sure how Alaric knew my shoe and dress size... Actually, maybe on second thought, I didn't want to know. I wouldn't put it past him to have someone measure me in my sleep. Regardless, both items fit perfectly. I absentmindedly pushed my fingers through my hair that was in need of a deep conditioning...or even a wash. The women's showers in this section of the prison were group showers, separated only by flimsy plastic curtains. I'd been walked in on multiple occasions so my showers tended to be as brief as humanly possible. Judging by the horror stories I heard about other sectors in the prison, I was lucky I got to shower at all.

But a girl could still dream about using nice shampoo.

As if Alaric could listen to my brain, another guard appeared at my cell door and opened it up, leaving again quickly after he set a nondescript brown box on the cot. Like the other two, he acted like I didn't exist.

Walking over to the box excitedly, I saw that it was full of various makeup products and a brush and mirror. This time, I didn't bother to hold in my squeal and couldn't have cared less about the curses that flew my direction.

I hadn't gotten a good look at my reflection since coming here. The showers had no mirrors, so my only view of myself had come from random reflections on pieces of metal and distorted images in the pools of filthy water that were all over the floors in this place. As I held up the mirror, I was surprised to see that besides looking pale from not seeing the sunlight...I looked good.

Better than ever actually.

My skin looked healthy and glowing, and the bags that had always been under my eyes were nowhere to be found, despite the fact that I hadn't gotten a good night's sleep since coming here. It must be something to do with my siren lineage.

I wasn't going to complain.

I took my time applying makeup, feeling a little bit myself again after having this time to primp. The guards here took an extreme amount of pleasure in making you feel almost like livestock. It was nice to get dressed up, even for one night. If I was allowed to keep the cosmetics and they weren't taken away in the random searches we were all periodically forced to endure, I still would rarely if ever use them again. It was best to fly under the radar as much as possible here, and my siren lineage made that difficult enough as it was. Despite the fact that the warden had taken my power, other siren attributes hadn't disappeared.

From what I'd seen, the guards were disgusting to the other prisoners, but their lecherousness seemed to hold new meaning when it came to me.

I shifted uncomfortably on my cot again, thinking of having to walk through the halls past prisoners and with a guard, dressed like this...

Maybe I should have said no.

Like an answer to a prayer, another mysterious guard appeared holding a garment bag. He set it down. This time, instead of disappearing, he stepped to the side as if he was waiting for me to exit the cell.

I unzipped the garment bag and saw a long black trench coat that while stylish, would hide my body from view from the top of my neck down to my ankles.

It was exactly what I needed.

I slipped it on and wasn't surprised that it fit like it had been made for me. I stood there awkwardly, not sure what I was supposed to do, since the guard hadn't said anything to me yet.

After a minute, when it became obvious I wasn't going to leave the cell without some kind of cue from him, he cleared his throat loudly.

I took that to be a signal I was supposed to leave my cell. He began walking immediately, not looking back to see if I was following him.

After hesitating for half a second, I stumbled behind him. It had been a minute since I'd worn shoes like this, and walking on an uneven floor on such high heels was a feat in and of itself.

Like usual, I didn't look into any of the cells we passed. It was enough to feel their interested stares. I'd made the mistake of looking in and meeting eyes with one of my cellmates my second week being here and had regretted it ever since then, as he had started to yell my prison number every time he came while he jacked off. Which was often.

I guess at least he wasn't calling out my name. The guards never bothered to call me that when they came to pick me up.

I was cursing my shoes five minutes into the journey. The guard kept up a brisk pace, not pausing at all, even when I tripped and almost fell. He led me through passages I'd never been through before, and I gasped when we slipped around the corner just as an enormous tail with giant spikes protruding out of it disappeared around a corner a few meters ahead. I shivered, thinking about the secrets this place held. Evidently, dragons were one of them.

At one point, I screamed as a huge spider the size of my head, the stuff of nightmares, came scuttling out of a hole in the wall, right in front of where we were about to walk. The guard even let out a brief grunt of surprise before he pulled a long broadsword out of his belt and sliced the thing's body in half. The legs continued to wriggle for a moment, and my whole body shook at the sight.

I was ready to go back to my cell. An assumedly nice dinner was not worth this. I was also eyeing the guard with increased trepidation, not knowing where exactly he had been hiding a sword that large. When he touched it to his belt, the sword seemed to just disappear.

Just another mystery I would have to ask Keon about. We really needed to spend more time talking and less time fucking. My list of things to ask about was a mile long at this point.

The spider had finally stopped moving, and the guard continued on as if nothing had happened. I gingerly stepped by the bug, keeping my body glued to the wall so I didn't have to step directly over him…just in case he deigned to come back to life and attack me. Although the wall probably wasn't safer, since the spider had come from the wall in the first place.

My nerves were shot at this point, and I began to curse Alaric's name with every nerve-racking step I took behind the guard. I kept a watchful gaze at the walls and up ahead, preparing myself for any more monsters to appear out of nowhere.

After I'd worked up a light sheen of sweat and was about ready to call the whole thing off, the guard stopped in front of me so suddenly that I almost ran into him. After the spider incident, I'd been trying to stay close, since he was the one with the weapons. I'm sure at this point, he was used to the dangers of this place and was prepared accordingly.

The guard finally locked eyes with me as he gave me an impatient look at my clumsiness. Before I could apologize, the wall in front of us disappeared, and whatever words I was about to say were gone in the face of the beauty in front of us.

It wasn't just Alaric dressed in a suit that had me awestruck—the whole room was magnificent. The walls were a deep emerald green color and were covered with silver sparkles, almost as if the walls were made completely of jewels.

And maybe they were. I'd never seen anything like it. My gaze traveled to the ceiling and my shock only grew. The ceiling had to be enchanted, like some sort of Harry Potter shit, because it literally looked like there was in fact no ceiling, and instead, we were outside under the night sky. And not just a normal sky, the kind that you could only see when you were out in the middle of nowhere, where there were so many stars visible that it was like the sky was covered in diamonds.

It could have been the most beautiful thing I'd ever seen.

But then Alaric stepped into my view again, and I really gave him a good look. Maybe he was actually the most beautiful thing I'd ever seen.

Elegant, yet sculpted in sharp lines, Alaric filled the seam of his tuxedo with a radiating sexuality. Full lips, a perfect smile…a jaw etched from stone, he was like every dream a woman had of what a man could look like.

I found myself staring wide-eyed at him, and I couldn't even bring myself to be embarrassed about it. My breath hitched as his intense gaze held mine for what felt like an eternity before his gaze started to drift down my body, still covered by the trench coat.

I felt woefully inadequate just then. He was perfect. And even in the sparkling clothes he'd given me, I didn't compare.

Taking a deep breath, I slowly unhooked my belt and opened the coat before letting it slip off my shoulders. His eyes returned to mine, continuing to weave whatever hypnotic spell he'd begun spinning the moment our gazes met.

"You look…" His voice faded off into a whisper, as if he'd lost the words. The emotion in his voice was enough for me, and I could feel a deep blush spreading in my cheeks and across my chest. I'd always been the type to blush with my entire body, and right now wasn't any different. It was probably worse. He shook his head, as if he was trying to gather his wits, and then strode towards me confidently and eager in a way that only made my blush deepen.

I looked over to see what the guard thought of this spectacle, but he was gone. It was just Alaric and me.

As soon as Alaric made it to me across the wide expanse of the room, he was in my personal space, pressed against me as close as humanly possible. His large hands engulfed my face as he pulled me in for a kiss. We kissed…long strokes that were hard and deep. His tongue played with mine, making me moan as I demanded more. I was still surprised at how fiercely my body reacted to his presence.

He tasted like *everything* I'd ever wanted or needed, and all I could think was that I wanted more…so much more. My fingers dove into his hair as we kissed, and even though we were as close together as possible, I pulled him forward even more, like I wanted to make him a part of me.

Alaric was finally the one to break our kiss and step away. A gratified look flashed in his gaze at the sound of discontentment that sparked out of me. His chest rose and fell sharply, as if he was barely hanging on to his control.

"I don't like being away from you too long," he said breathlessly, before pushing his hair out of his face and taking a deep inhale as he tried to collect himself. "As much as I want more of your mouth on mine…much more in fact, I did invite you for the purpose of a date." His lips smirked deliciously, and I was prepared to forget dinner and move onto dessert at that moment.

As if he saw I was about to jump him, Alaric turned and clapped his hands three times. A panel in the wall across from us opened, and an actual suit-wearing waiter stepped into the room, holding a black tray with two silver domes.

Alaric turned back towards me, looking much calmer now, and held out his arm for me to take. It was the most gentleman-like thing I'd ever seen from him. The butterflies in my stomach sparked up even more. There was a table for two draped in a rich, black fabric just beyond Alaric. I'd been so caught up with him and the rest of the room that I hadn't even noticed it. The waiter set up a stand next to the table and set the tray on top of it, deftly removing the silver lids and revealing plates with what looked like a smorgasbord of various appetizers. Alaric led me to one of the chairs and pulled out my seat so that I could sit down. He kissed my cheek as I scooted closer to the table, and I was barely able to withhold the moan that was threatening to come out just from the brush of his lips against my skin. I shook my head as images of his lips traveling down other parts of my skin barreled through my thoughts. I flushed even deeper as Alaric sat down and shot me a knowing smile, as if he could see the racy images in my mind right now.

The waiter set one of the plates in front of me, and this time, a moan did come out at the delicious smell emanating from the platter. The food in the prison was disgusting, despite what my cockatrice friend thought, and there hadn't been a time where my stomach hadn't turned from smelling my meals as they were either brought to my cell or taken in the mess hall.

The smell coming off the food in front of me had the opposite effect. I thought it smelled even better than Alaric did…and that was saying something. I didn't even think before picking up my fork and digging in. Alaric continued to watch me with a satisfied gleam in his gaze as I feasted on crab cakes, artichoke and spinach dip, bacon wrapped chestnuts, and steak bites that were so good, I wanted to cry in happiness.

I didn't stop until every morsel was gone, and even then, I was tempted to lick the plate. Despite the fact that Alaric had been staring at me the whole time, he managed to finish off his plate just a little after I did. The waiter was quick to appear from the side of the room to get our empty plates.

"This chef does spectacular work," Alaric commented as he wiped his lips with the silk napkin from the table.

"I think that was the best thing I've ever eaten," I gushed. "How in the world did you manage to do all of this? How did you get a chef, and my dress…and everything else?"

Alaric smirked, the infuriating smirk this time, which announced to anybody who saw it that he knew things you didn't. "I have my ways," he drawled. I picked up my fork and mimicked stabbing him with it.

"You have to give me more than that," I demanded with a pout.

Alaric grabbed my fork and spun it around on his fingers as he stared at me thoughtfully. It felt like he was measuring me up, deciding how much I could take. I sat up straighter in my chair, only faintly noticing the waiter setting a mouth-watering salad in front of me.

Alaric waited until the waiter had disappeared behind the wall before speaking. "What have you heard about the southern territories, how they are run?" he asked as he continued to stare at me contemplatively.

"The southern territories?" I asked, confused. "They're the only territories not controlled by Julian and his crew, I at least know that. They have some sort of warlord leader." I pursed my lips trying to remember the whisperings I'd heard. I'd known that Julian despised the leader in the southern territories, despised and almost feared him at times.

I focused back on Alaric and saw that his smug grin was back, wider than ever. My brain was slow to connect the dots. "Are you from the southern territories?"

His grin grew even wider. He gave me back my fork and picked up his own as he began to nonchalantly eat his salad. After chewing his bite, he finally answered. "I am."

I growled. "If you don't stop being so fucking secretive, I really am going to leave," I threatened.

He rolled his eyes, as if that was impossible. Which maybe it was. I wasn't sure that I could make that long trip in these heels again. I would have to go barefoot, and who knew what kind of disease I would get from doing that.

"I'm the leader of the southern territories," he answered after another excruciatingly long pause while he chewed another bite of salad.

I dropped my fork that I'd just picked up. "The warlord?" I gasped. Everything I'd heard came rushing back into my mind. He was known to be bloodthirsty, ruthless, a beast whose cruelty put the vampires to shame.

He watched me warily now. "It appears that you've heard some stories," he commented dryly.

I nodded, a slice of fear churned through my gut. I'd had sex with him. I knew he had to be dangerous, but this was a level of danger I hadn't contemplated.

"Those stories…are they true?" I asked hesitantly.

His eyes darkened as he stared at me. I could see the savageness clearly now. He'd kept it hidden from me for the most part. "Many of them. You don't become a king in this world without the spilling of blood."

"And how exactly did you end up here?" I asked, finally giving in to my still growling stomach to stab at some lettuce. In danger or not, I was going to at least have one last fantastic meal.

"Voluntarily of course," he answered, amused at my question.

"Voluntarily?"

"Yes. There are things I'm looking for here, that if I find them, will mean that our territory will never be challenged again." His words were vague, but he said just enough for me to know who he was talking about.

"The warden has something you want," I said with a sigh, understanding now why he wasn't going to waste his break-in on something for Seth when he had his eyes on something for himself. "How do you know you won't lose your territory anyway while you're in here?" I asked, thinking of how lawless I'd heard the Southern territories were.

He snorted as if I said the funniest thing possible. "What?" I asked defensively. "Power isn't absolute."

"Mine might as well be," he commented with absolute surety. "I have lieutenants in place, beasts who are bound to me and aren't able to, nor would they want to, usurp me.

I had so many more questions.

Just then, the waiter appeared. "Was the salad not to your liking, Miss?" he asked as he picked up Alaric's empty plate and eyed my still full one.

I looked at my plate glumly. "It was perfect," I sighed.

"Just leave it there and bring out the next course," Alaric ordered, waving the waiter away. The waiter scurried off without a look back.

Alaric reached across the table and grabbed my hand. He pulled me forward, placing my hand over his heart. "You don't ever have to be afraid of me," he told me fiercely. "I would rather die than ever hurt you."

I eyed him, emotion welling up in my throat at the sincerity in his voice. Alaric was powerful...strong... elusive. And the way that he was looking at me was as if he needed me more than air.

"Selena," he growled in a gravelly voice. A flush spread across my chest again at the intensity in his voice as he said my name.

Before I could say anything in return, the waiter appeared, carrying a heaping tray covered in plates of steaming food. Alaric looked like he wanted to kill the waiter for the interruption, but luckily, he held himself back.

The waiter set down a tray of creamy pasta and a platter of sliced steak covered in some sort of green sauce. There was a plate of perfectly golden browned rolls, another plate filled with glazed carrots in an abundance of colors, and a bowl full of perfectly whipped mashed potatoes.

I was in heaven.

"Let's table the more serious talk and eat all of this," suggested Alaric. I eagerly agreed, not wanting to waste a speck of the incredible feast before us.

We ate, and we talked. And it was wonderful, all of it. All serious talk was put aside, and instead, Alaric regaled me with stories about growing up and his family and his lieutenants back home, who seemed more like family than friends with the affectionate way he talked about them.

He tried to ask me questions, but I turned the attention back to him every time. My history was a tapestry of despair, and I didn't want to ruin the fun we were having with stories about that. That could come another time.

It was amazing, all the different sides to Alaric. There were different sides to everyone, but no one I knew held them so close to the chest as Alaric did.

Alaric was so lighthearted throughout the meal, it was like I was dining with a different person. I should have wished that this was who he was all the time, but something was obviously wrong with me. As much I was attracted to this version of him, I craved the darker part of him.

After stuffing more than what three people should probably eat in a day into my stomach, I set down my fork and leaned back in my chair. "I can't eat another bite," I groaned. "And how am I ever going to go back to the slop they serve in this place when I know food like this exists in the world?"

Alaric laughed. It was deep and genuine, warming me from the inside out. I wished I was funnier so I could make him laugh like that all the time.

"I'm positive I could make this happen again," he said happily, like my enjoyment was all he wanted. "But are you sure you are too full for another bite? I'm pretty sure that dessert is worth breaking that pledge."

I perked up in my seat immediately. Dessert wasn't really something that Rosalind believed in. Even though sirens were biologically created to maintain an appealing figure, Rosalind had always firmly believed that one couldn't be too careful. I hadn't tasted chocolate until my seventeenth birthday, when Julian had presented me with a giant chocolate cake.

My heart flipped just then, remembering that chocolate cake.

Julian was the villain in my story. I hated him, but at some point, part of me had probably loved him in the way that only a child starving for affection from someone could love. He had taken that love and twisted it into something so dark and terrible, that now, all that was left was hate.

"Selena?" Alaric asked gently, staring at me in concern.

I shook my head, as if that would get rid of all the memories, and flashed him a real smile. Dessert. I could definitely do dessert with him.

While the waiter grabbed our plates and the rest of the dishes on the table, Alaric stood up and grabbed my hand, walking me over to a large settee set up against one of the emerald walls. Right before I tried to sit down, he scooped me up in his arms and settled down on the couch while he snuggled me into his lap.

Like the attention-starved woman that I was, I reveled in the affection he was giving me.

Our other encounters had been hot. Scorching really. But as much as I'd loved and craved those, I needed this. The waiter silently brought over a tray of chocolate-covered strawberries and a bucket of ice with a fancy looking bottle of champagne in it.

Alaric picked up one of the strawberries and brought it up to my mouth. He stared at me, fascinated, as I opened my mouth and took a bite. I could feel chocolate smeared along my upper lip, and before I could clean it off, Alaric licked it off.

Somehow, it was extremely sexy. I was feeling a little breathless as Alaric pulled away from me. He made sure to act like he was savoring the chocolate in his mouth, knowing exactly what it was doing to me. Alaric reached for the two glasses of champagne that the waiter had poured.

"What's our waiter's name?" I asked, suddenly realizing how rude it was that I didn't know it and had been referring to him as "waiter" in my head this whole time, when he had been serving us for a few hours.

"Johnny something or other," Alaric mused dismissively. "He's the son of one of our suppliers in the next town over. He leaped at the chance to do this."

Somehow, I doubted that anyone "leaped" at the chance to visit Nightmare Penitentiary. I mean, there was always the risk that you wouldn't make it out of here. I let the matter drop though. I didn't really care. Alaric was too distracting.

I took a gulp of my champagne, hoping for some liquid courage, since the wine I'd had at dinner had only provided so much. "This thing you are hoping to get from the warden—"

"Going to get from the warden," Alaric corrected me confidently. I rolled my eyes.

"Going to get from the warden. Wait—should we be talking about this so openly? He has eyes everywhere," I fretted, staring around us suspiciously, like I was going to see the warden hidden in the walls.

"It's a little late to worry about that, isn't it?" commented Alaric wryly.

I shrugged sheepishly.

"I'm sure the warden knows exactly why I'm here. I think he thinks this is some kind of game. To see who will prevail," Alaric mused.

"You really think he knows?"

"Like you said, he has eyes everywhere. One doesn't

simply 'catch' me," he said with a laugh. "I'm just biding my time."

"What are you waiting for?" I asked, frowning as I thought about Alaric leaving this place—and me— behind. My heart seemed like it was being squeezed inside my chest at the thought. I rubbed my chest, trying to get rid of the achy feeling.

"What do you think I'm waiting for?" Alaric answered intensely as he gazed into my eyes.

My mouth floundered in shock.

"Don't think for a moment that I will be leaving these walls without you," he told me fervently. The squeeze on my heart abruptly quit, and something that felt like elation coursed through me.

Unbidden images of Keon…and Seth…appeared in my mind just then.

"I have things I have to do here as well," I told Alaric seriously, and he nodded, unsurprised, like he knew all about my plans. And maybe he did.

"Don't make me wait too long, my queen," he murmured. And I knew the threat in his voice didn't mean that he would leave without me if I took too long. It meant that he would take me with him no matter if I was done with what I needed to do or not.

And somehow, that didn't bother me as much as it should have.

"You called me 'queen,'" I commented, noting that was the first time he'd called me something like that.

"Because you will be my queen when I return home. No one will ever threaten you or harm you again. You will be esteemed above all others." His words were a promise that called to me.

But again, Keon and Seth's faces appeared in my head.

"Don't think about them," Alaric growled, pulling my chin so that I had no choice but to look at him. "When you're here with me, I'm the only one you're thinking about." His possessiveness wrapped around me like a heavy cloak, and I reveled in it.

It was like he could see all the broken, discarded parts inside of me and knew exactly what to do to put them back together. His kiss was frantic when our lips met this time. It was hot and demanded everything from me, even though I had nothing to give. Through his kiss, feelings of inadequacy and insecurity from the past I couldn't let go of floated away, until there was absolutely no thoughts of them anywhere.

Tightly bound control slipped as he licked and bit into my mouth, driving pleasure from the piercing sting, until my cry rebounded against the gleaming jewel-like walls. I was completely at his mercy. With his silent insistence, I accepted my fate and dove in. I wrapped my arms around his head, my fingers plunged into his hair, and I pulled him closer, matching him need for need.

There was only him.

There was only us.

And it almost felt like it could be like this forever.

"I'm lost in you," he whispered as his lips began a slow, painful descent down my neck.

"I want to possess you...mark you...come all over you so you carry my scent with you always. Make sure everyone knows you belong to me." His voice was rough and thick. He licked up my pulse point and pinched my nipple hard through my thin dress, sending a spasm spiraling through me.

"Yes," I breathed, amazed at how much I wanted his dirty words and the dark promises he was giving me.

Alaric's touch was pure temptation, seductive as he peeled off my dress and then ripped off my underwear. He set me down on the settee and stood up, staring down at me hungrily. He began to strip off his clothes slowly, and my mouth watered as inch by inch of his gold, glorious skin appeared for my viewing pleasure.

He stripped until there was nothing left that would separate him from me. He picked me up so that we were skin against skin. Enfolded in his arms, he worshipped my mouth with his, and my body heated under his touch as he caressed every whispered shadow. He captured my groan, taking it in to mix with his. I whimpered as he kissed across my cheek to my ear and down my neck, nibbling at the hollow above my collarbone.

My hands moved...they were everywhere. His shoulders, arms, running over the hard lines of his back. Everything he did taunted the wicked pulse between my thighs that had been slowly building throughout the night.

Without warning, he set me back down on the

settee, pushing me gently back until I was lying down on it.

He didn't follow though.

His breath faltered as he gazed down at me.

Slow and deliberate, his inspection of my naked body was thorough, and his voice was rough when he spoke.

"I want you. Just the thought of you gets me hard."

I couldn't help but stare at his rock-hard erection. His hand followed my eyes, stroking up and down. He was magnificent. As he stood there, it seemed like a glittery gold mist appeared around him, somehow heightening my lust.

Was this his power?

"Seeing you spread out before me, wanting me as much as I want you…it's almost too much," he groaned, and I watched as his eyes seemed to change.

The passionate need was replaced with veneration, a worshiping glint as he drank me in.

"My queen," he breathed into the silence, the title a prayer on his lips. Slowly, he laid next to me, a tight fit for sure, bringing a hand up to cup the full weight of my breast. Closing his eyes, he leaned in so that his mouth hovered over mine, not touching, just taking.

It was beyond intimate, his almost touching, but I was desperate to kiss him.

"Alaric," I whispered breathlessly, and the word broke whatever spell we were under. His eyes opened, a devilish gleam replacing the adoration. He pinched my nipple, pulling it until I moaned. The sweet sensation drove straight down to my groin, a sharp, inescapable fluttering. He smiled, a slow, beguiling grin as I writhed beneath his dark stare and the attention of his fingers.

"I'm going to taste you, my queen. Lick and bite you until you scream my name."

My mouth formed a perfect O, but I said nothing, paralyzed with anticipation. I watched as he dipped down, taking me into his mouth, laving the elongated tip of my breast with his tongue before teasing it between his teeth. I leaned back into the couch cushion. I reeled from the pleasure his mouth brought. One at a time, he played with my breasts until I was wet and hungry for him.

"Please," I begged for the pleasure I knew he could give me. The gold mist intensified, and his pupils were blown in arousal, threatening to overtake the beautiful steel grey of his eyes. Nonsensical words flowed from my mouth as I begged him to continue, to keep touching me, for him to bring an end to the burning need building between my thighs.

Slowly he moved, in no hurry to stop my torture. His nose trailed along my skin, teasing a path until he pressed into me, groaning as he breathed deeply, as if my scent was his favorite thing he'd ever experienced. I blushed again at the intimate gesture.

Eyes trained on mine, he pushed my thighs slowly apart. "You're intoxicating." His voice was hot, his breath hotter as he blew against me. Looking up through his lashes, he asked, "Do you want this, Selena? Tell me you need this as much as I do."

I was speechless, so he blew against me again.

"Say it. I need to hear you," he ordered sharply, and my body immediately bent to his will.

"Yes," I barely breathed out before his head dipped, the tip of his tongue swirling around my clitoris. My body arched off the cushions at the sweet carnal sensation, and I moaned loudly. Closing my eyes, I focused on him and the tormenting flick of his tongue. Wrapping his arms under my hips, he became impassioned, groaning as he lifted me to his mouth.

I couldn't move, my only outlet the words continuing to fall almost soundlessly into the still air as I begged him for more and praised him for his efforts. Clenching my hands into the cushion, I surrendered to the beautiful intensity, panting.

"Alaric," I cried out. An errant thought slipped through my lustful fog that I hoped that no one was listening in. Alaric had a way about him that never failed to make me forget my surroundings.

His lips closed around my clitoris, and my brain went blank again, as he sucked and rolled it between his teeth. I arched and instinctively moved with him, a wicked, slow dance that I never wanted to end. The music was his mouth, playing artfully, and all I could do was wait, longing for the crescendo.

Releasing my death grip on the cushion beneath me, I grabbed the soft silk of his hair as his head swayed between my thighs. He looked up, eyes scorching and erotic, his tongue insistent and hot, teasing but not taking me over the edge.

"Please," I whimpered again, begging for the push from the burning plateau. His answer was to slide a finger inside my welcoming body. I groaned again. The longing and desire built, the friction of his finger along with his mouth took me higher, faster than I thought possible. I writhed against him, the dance becoming feverish. All I was was burning need.

"Don't stop," I growled this time, the words coming out almost animalistic in their intensity.

Two fingers plunged into me once, twice. His tongue flicked and rolled again and again, and he launched me beyond the brink. I exploded, screaming out in awe as the crescendo hit violently. Waves of pleasure crashed through my entire body, and I bowed into him once more. His mouth and fingers continued to move on me, in me, pushing my orgasm on and on. When I could stand it no more, I tugged his hair, pulling him up to me. Diving into his mouth, I tasted myself on his tongue, relishing the feel of his lips stroking over mine.

Without thought, I grabbed his bottom lip between my teeth, sucking on it, mimicking what he just did to me. Drinking in his low moan, I spurred him on for more.

"Need something, my queen?" he taunted me.

"I want you," I answered fiercely, moving suddenly so that I was the one on top. I just barely managed to avoid falling to the floor with my eagerness.

"What do you need?" he teased me again.

All I could answer with was a growl as I pulled him to me. In one swift move, I impaled myself on him, crying out as my body acclimated to the invasion.

His erection reached inside of me in a new way, a full tormenting stretch that had me forgetting everything else about my existence. We groaned together when I rotated my hips, deepening the penetration. Our eyes locked, the intensity staggering. Leaning down, I placed my hands on either side of his face, cradling him tenderly. My mouth hovered over his, not touching, just taking. Taking him into me every way I knew how.

His breath, his body, we became one, and I began to make love with Alaric for the first time. A sweet, beautiful, passionate love that I hadn't known we were capable of.

I felt it all. I felt all of him.

My hips moved, rounding gently at first, pulling him in and out at a taunting, tortuous pace. Our breath mingled together, held tight against us as our bodies joined, again and again, over and over. In time, I pushed up, sitting on him fully so he sank in further, a new humbling depth that had us both groaning again in unison. Our rhythm changed. We needed...we wanted... We moved passionately against each other again and again.

The joy in this moment, in us, was achingly sweet. Who knew that the sweetest moments of my life would somehow come amongst the worst?

"Alaric," I whispered again as our eyes met, his that striking steel grey I'd never seen on another being. I'm sure mine looked confused, bewildered by the staggering emotion I felt at this moment to this man who should never have been mine.

My thoughts scattered, frayed with unbridled tension, and I dissolved around him, mind and body surrendering to the mystifying connection. I cried out as his hips pushed me higher, rocketing with him, trusting in wherever he wanted to take me, and I came. I erupted around him, vaguely hearing his cry as he joined me. We were one—we were us.

My breath shattered, I fell, splayed out on his chest. His hands wrapped into my hair, holding me tight as our bodies calmed.

Eventually, he pulled my lips to his, kissing me gently. We breathed into each other, sated.

Eventually, I fell asleep.

And when I woke up, I was back in my cell, dressed once again in my ugly prison issued jumpsuit, like it had all been a dream.

Only the pulsing ache in between my legs and the silver dress that was tightly gripped in my hand told me it had all been real.

And I didn't know what to do with that.

CHAPTER 8

SELENA

The next day, I felt off. That was the only way to describe it. I fluctuated between being glad that I had space to absorb what had happened last night, and needing to see Alaric or Keon to confirm that everything between us hadn't been my imagination.

Today, a guard had informed me it was a mess hall day, and now I found myself floating through the room to get into line, not paying much attention to my surroundings.

Which was always a dangerous thing to do in a place like this.

"Siren," a deep and familiar voice whispered in my ear from behind me. I jumped as I swirled around, only breathing a small sigh of relief when I saw that it was the hellhound shifter.

I really should find out his name.

My heart began to beat rapidly in my chest, and I

couldn't tell if it was because I was scared of him, or because of how good he looked… Maybe it was a little of both.

"Hello," I answered awkwardly. He seemed to always be here when I was here. Which was odd in and of itself. The prison kept the mess hall schedule random so that fights couldn't be pre-planned. Which made sense. If you didn't know when you were going to be somewhere, and you didn't know who would be there with you, it followed that you couldn't exactly plan out how to shank someone.

Which made the fact that the hellhound was always here strange. I hadn't noticed anyone else who had been in the mess hall at the same time as me even twice. And somehow, he managed to be here every time.

"What are they serving today?" he asked conversationally as he grabbed a tray for me and then one for himself.

"Thank you," I said politely as I took the tray, ignoring the fluttering feeling I got when his fingers brushed against mine.

It had to be the fact that I was having so much sex here. Keon and Alaric were keeping me in a constantly sexed-up state of mind, and that was the cause of the fluttery feeling. It couldn't possibly be anything else.

At least, that was what I told myself.

"Looks like the usual slop," I answered as I looked in disgust at the grey colored stew that one of the workers was serving up to prisoners just ahead of me.

My stomach panged at the memory of the delicious dinner from the night before. I still had suspicions that last night was a dream… There was no way it could have actually been that good.

I winced as some of the grey matter splashed onto the front of my shirt as the worker sloshed the stew onto my tray. Looking ahead, I was relieved to see that there were some apples left in the fruit bowl. At least I would have something to eat, because I was pretty sure that this stuff would kill me if I ate it.

I grabbed the apple and headed to a table on the far side of the room that was empty, very aware that the hellhound was following me. I sat down at the table and ignored him as he sat directly across from me.

"My name is Laz by the way," he told me cheerfully.

"Laz?"

"Short for Lazarus. My mother had a thing for biblical stories," he explained as he took a big bite of the stew and then grimaced, looking a little green as he dutifully swallowed it. "I wouldn't eat that if I were you."

I snorted. "I didn't plan on it," I told him as I bit into my apple. The apple had a few brown spots, but all in all, it didn't taste that bad. I'd also managed to snag a slice of carrot cake, one of the only desserts that was edible in the mess hall. Hopefully, that would tide me over until the next meal that I could stomach here.

Laz sniffed his apple warily before carefully biting into it. It must have been alright, because he proceeded to munch away. "So, what are you in here for?" he asked casually, making me choke on the bite of apple I'd just taken.

"Refusing to sleep with my vampire overlord and then giving my virginity up to a stranger," I said straight-faced.

Laz's jaw dropped…as did his apple, landing with a splash in his stew…which went everywhere.

"Fuck, why would you joke about something like that?" he moaned as he tried to wipe himself off with a napkin. I was just lucky that none of it had landed on me. As it was, I would have to scrub my uniform in the sink from what had splashed on it earlier. I didn't want to spend the day smelling like dirty socks.

"I wasn't joking," I told him as I lifted an eyebrow.

He stuttered for a second before I took pity on him. "It's okay," I said with a sigh. "I wouldn't have believed that story either if I hadn't lived it."

He shook his head, and there was a heavy awkwardness between us. I could feel anger wafting off of him. I couldn't decide what was making him angry. Surely, it wasn't about my situation. That was a lot of anger to feel about a stranger's predicament. I'm sure there were a lot of innocents in this place with stories to tell. Maybe not quite like mine, but probably equally terrible.

As far as I was concerned, any story that involved an innocent person ending up in this place was a terrible tragedy. I didn't think most of them had a prison mouse and men like Alaric, Keon…and Seth, I belatedly added, to keep them company.

"That's fucking terrible," he finally said. "I knew you were a siren, but I didn't know the rest of your story."

I moved around uncomfortably in my seat. His kindness felt like it was too much. I still wasn't used to others being kind at all, much less in a place like this.

"It hasn't been so bad," I told him, reaching out and tentatively patting the top of his hand, which was clenched tightly on top of the table. "Really. It's probably better than what my life was out there."

He finally pulled up his head and looked at me, and the empathy in his gaze threatened to overwhelm me. We just stared at each other for a long moment. I opened my mouth to ask him what he was in for, it only seemed fair that he had to tell me now, when suddenly, the crowd in the mess hall quieted.

Two burly guards had entered the room, the looks on their faces like they were just daring the prisoners to bring trouble.

"Selena Alexander," the guard on the left barked, looking around the room. I shakily stood up, knowing that these guards weren't here to give me a surprise from Alaric.

Laz had stood up as well and looked ready to run at the guards if I asked him too. I shot him what I hoped looked like a reassuring smile, and shook my head briefly to signal to him that I didn't want him to do anything.

Catcalls broke out as I began to walk towards the guards who were watching me wickedly, as if I was about to drop down on my knees in front of them. I heard a snarl behind me that I knew belonged to Laz, but I didn't look back. I didn't want to get him in trouble.

"Pick up the pace, Ms. Alexander," the guard on the right snarled as his hand twitched by his side, like he was just itching to pick out one of the weapons attached around his belt. I hurried my stride, taking a deep breath right before I reached them to calm myself down.

The guard grabbed my arm tightly, and I winced, knowing I would have a handprint shaped bruise on my arm there later on. Asshole.

Another growl broke out behind me, and the second that we stepped out of the room, it was like the whole room went insane. I looked back as I was frog-marched away to see most of the prisoners attacking each other. Evidently, their inability to fight their oppressors meant that the only way they could get the aggression out was to attack each other.

I sent up a silent prayer that Laz would be alright, when I heard what sounded like a dog yelp in pain somewhere in the crowd.

But maybe I should have been praying for myself.

The guards were silent. Their menacing presence seemed to take up the whole hallway, and it wasn't the respectful silence of the guards that Alaric had sent to my cell with gifts.

It was the kind of silence where you're just holding your breath and hoping that everything turns out okay and the monsters don't appear out of the shadows.

I didn't know whether to be relieved or frightened when I realized that they were taking me to the warden's office. Surely, he couldn't have expected me to have found out where the scepter was hidden already? He'd been beating Seth to the brink of death daily, and the guy was not inclined to trust anyone... for good reason.

A guilty pang reverberated through my chest. He definitely shouldn't trust me.

All thoughts of Seth faded away as I stepped into the warden's office. He was standing in front of one of his bookshelves, the one that held my glowing orb of power actually. I closed my eyes for a second, enjoying the pulsating waves of power that I could feel, even across the room. It had taken me a bit to recognize it, and now I couldn't miss it whenever I was summoned by the warden.

Someday, I was going to have it back and be whole. Someday.

"Selena, so nice of you to join me today," the warden remarked without looking back at me.

A wave of unease flickered down my spine. "Did you need something?" I asked blandly, not knowing what else to say but too annoyed to be more polite.

At my tone, he finally turned around. He was in all black today, and the effect was frankly foreboding. He stalked towards me, and I struggled not to cower in fear. He changed course at the last second, gliding behind his desk, as if that had been his intention all along. My hands shook beside me, and I clasped them tightly together in an effort to hide my fear.

The warden's smile told me that I hadn't succeeded.

"What do you think I need, my little siren?" he asked pointedly.

"It's barely been any time at all," I responded defensively, my throat coming out raspy from the fear that was coating my insides.

"My guards say that you haven't made any progress at all." He lifted an eyebrow as if daring me to argue with him.

"I wouldn't say that," I responded hesitantly and sat down on the seat across the desk from him. "I'm building his trust. Torturing him every day hasn't exactly made my job easy."

He stood up from his chair slowly, leaning over his desk so that he was towering over me. I forced myself to keep my spine straight, even though the dark waves of power emanating out of him demanded that I cower.

"Maybe I didn't make myself clear last time exactly what my expectations were. I don't want you to become his friend. I want you to get his secrets. I don't care if that means that you have to hang him by his fingernails to get them. YOU WILL GET THEM!" His voice came out in a roar. Other voices were threaded with his voice, a million demons joining him as he made sure to get the point across.

Tears were streaming down my face from the force of his power. I felt something wet under my nose. Wiping what I thought was snot off my face, I was surprised to see that my hand was smeared with blood. It became clear to me that despite what he'd said about my freedom being at stake if I did not get him what he wanted…it was actually my life that was at stake.

The warden suddenly jerked his hand up, and my body flew out of my chair, crashing against the back wall so forcefully that a bookshelf nearby crashed forward from the impact.

Which only made the warden even angrier. Again, he moved his hand up, and I flew off the ground where I had laid crumpled, and once again, was smashed against the wall, shaking the entire room with the force of my impact. I lay strewn on the floor, pain coursing through every part of my body.

The warden always seemed to be controlled before this. Dangerous and deadly, yes. But controlled. None of his control was present anymore. His anger was tinged with desperation—the most dangerous form of anger, I'd always believed. It was a little far-fetched to believe that his desire to help out the light fae would lead to this kind of reaction.

What exactly did he want that scepter for…?

The warden took a deep breath, squeezing the bridge of his nose as he tried to calm down. My whole body ached. Recovering from this was going to be killer. I was pretty sure that he'd broken some of the vertebrae in my back. If I was any lesser of a creature, I would have been paralyzed.

I struggled to stand up from the floor where I'd landed after the crash against the wall. I could feel my spinal cord struggling to weave itself back together inside of me. Blood was gushing out of my nose copiously at this point. I wheezed as I pushed myself up. Evidently, I'd punctured one of my lungs as well. I fell back to the floor, unable to keep myself standing.

Too bad the nurse here was insane. I probably could have used some medical attention right about now.

The warden watched me, looking like he was taking pleasure from my agony. "I think we need something a bit more to drive the point home about how important this task is, Selena. Don't you?"

I struggled to try and find something to say. How was what he'd just done not enough?

"Braden," the warden snapped, and the guard appeared that had brought me to the office. "Take her to our special prisoner's cell."

"Yes, sir," the guard replied immediately. My stomach sank ominously.

Who was the special prisoner? And how would this be part of my punishment?

The guard hauled me up from the ground as roughly as he could, causing me to almost pass out from the pain.

"I want to see results," the warden called out after us as I was dragged out of the room. I heard something crash against the wall in the office after we got out into the hallway.

Something was definitely not right about all of this.

I couldn't worry about the warden's intentions for long though, because with how rough the guard was being with me, I wasn't sure I would make it long enough to have to worry about what the warden wanted from me.

Every time we rounded a corner, the guard made sure to slam me against the stone wall as we turned. My arms more closely resembled ground hamburger meat than they did human skin as the journey went along. I didn't bother asking him who the "special prisoner" was. I had a feeling that this guard wasn't about to tell me the answer.

I couldn't walk, and the guard obviously wasn't keen on carrying me in his arms, so I was basically dragged along beside him. The ground was the furthest thing from clean, and I knew I was looking at an infection in all my wounds…if the guard didn't kill me first.

Maybe the "special prisoner" was some sort of monster that they tortured prisoners with here. Maybe it was that beast whose tail I'd seen walking to dinner with Alaric the other night.

It was funny that I'd actually felt like this place wasn't so bad because of Alaric and Keon. This place was a nightmare.

I heard his screams when we were still a ways out. There were always a lot of screams in this place—people were miserable after all—but I knew whose screams these were.

Seth.

We had come in a back way, so I hadn't recognized where we were going, not to mention I had blood dripping down my face, so my vision wasn't as clear as usual.

But there was no mistaking the sound of his pain.

He was usually silent, only occasionally did the pain become so much that he made a sound. The fact that he was full on screaming meant that whatever was being done to him was on a whole other level than the torture he was usually subjected to.

I realized then that this was my lesson. He was the "special prisoner."

I hadn't imagined that it would be a worse punishment to watch someone else be tortured and not myself, but in this case, it was.

I was only faintly aware of my own injuries as he came into view. Seth was hanging by his hands from the ceiling, his toes barely dragging on the floor. Both of his arms were clearly out of socket from the position. There were three guards gathered around him. Instead of the whip I'd seen them with in the past, this time, they were each holding a whip that had spikes protruding from it.

Each time the spike hit Seth, his skin shredded. The carnage was so bad that strips of his skin were hanging off his back. I'd never seen anything like it. I gagged when the whip struck again and chunks of bloody flesh flew off his back, showering his cell.

At some point, Seth passed out.

And still, they kept going.

I began to beg for mercy, offering anything they

wanted for them to stop. But none of the guards even looked at me.

They had their orders, and nothing I did was going to change their mind.

I tried to watch, wanting to absorb the horror and pain that I was responsible for, but after a time, it became too much and I had to close my eyes. I kept them closed until the snap of the whips stopped and the clang of Seth's cell opening alerted me that the session was over.

The guards left me there in the hallway, Seth's cell door open in front of me, taunting me, since I couldn't move at the moment.

I lay there, staring at Seth's prone form. And I think that was worse torture than my body as it tried to knit itself together…which wasn't going very successfully.

After what seemed like an eternity, but was probably only an hour, he stirred. The guards had left him on the ground facing me, so our eyes immediately met when he opened them. We both just stared at each other, so many things written in the depths of our gazes.

"I'm sorry," I croaked, the words woefully inadequate for the sorrow in my heart.

"I know," he answered. And I liked that he didn't just say it wasn't my fault. I liked that he finally let me own up to this terrible thing that had just happened to him.

My body had healed just enough for me to drag myself forward. I kept going until I was next to him, even though my body protested every agonizingly slow movement.

"I would have done anything to prevent this," I swore to him, knowing the words were true. Somewhere along these past weeks, I'd grown to care for him in such a way that I would bring on any pain that lay ahead of me if it meant that I could protect him.

How did that even happen? I'd had my goals here. I'd had my mission from the warden, a way out of here with a chance at getting back what I'd thought I wanted the most in the world—my power back. And somehow, here I was, knowing that I would sacrifice whatever he needed to help him, even if it did cost me my life like the warden had warned.

Hearts were a fickle, stupid thing.

I hated Seth just as much as I cared for him at that moment.

Because right then, I knew that I was giving up my chance of freedom.

Stupid, stupid heart.

I felt a brush against my face. I hadn't realized I was crying, but there Seth was, catching one of my tears tenderly, even in his miserable state. His hands trembled against my face, and I leaned into his touch, hating myself even as I soaked in every second of comfort he was willing to give me.

"I'm not sorry..." he began, before coughing hard, a trickle of blood coming out of his mouth. He took a wheezy breath and then tried again. "I don't mind the beatings anymore. They barely hurt. I think they're losing their touch." He tried to smile, but it ended up a bit macabre, as his teeth were stained with blood.

"How can you say that?" I cried, more tears falling from my face.

"Because they mean that I get to see you. No matter what happens, I'll never regret getting to see you."

He leaned forward, and his lips barely brushed against mine. But it was enough. Enough to make my soul feel like it was bursting. Enough for me to feel like the sun had suddenly appeared and it was shining down on me. His lips pressed against mine again, this time with more pressure, and it was almost too much. I could taste the metallic tang of our blood, but it somehow only heightened the promises we were giving each other in that kiss. A small moan escaped my lips. The kiss was deep and long, and it seemed to go on forever and still wasn't enough.

I didn't think that any number of kisses would've been enough.

I finally pulled away when the guilt of what I'd done shot me through the heart once more.

"I'm sorry," he said, and I laughed a sort of crazed kind of laugh, because this beautiful, perfect fae was actually apologizing to me.

"Don't ever apologize to me. Especially not for kissing me. That was perfect," I reassured him.

My injuries started to creep up on me just then. It felt like a jackhammer had taken up residence in my head and had gone to work.

I wasn't sure if we both passed out or fell asleep, but

I didn't come back into awareness until I woke up in the medical wing, a crazed looking Dr. Brina standing over me with a scalpel that I knew instantly I didn't want anywhere near my body.

I quickly scurried up my bed, prepared to climb up the wall if it meant getting away from the scalpel wielding psycho in front of me.

Huh. I was moving. And the pain was nothing compared to what my injuries had been.

How long had I been here to gain that much progress? And what had happened to Seth?

"I'm good, thanks," I hurriedly said when she continued to advance on me. I don't think I'd ever seen so much crazy in a person's eyes. She could give the warden a run for his money on the whole fear factor thing. I think I would take the warden over Dr. Brina any day.

I sneezed when her Chance Chanel perfume hit me, once again reminding me of my mother. Besides the fact that Dr. Brina was a creep, I had disliked her from the beginning. That hadn't changed after the stunt she had pulled the last time I needed medical attention. I still remembered clearly the scrape of her teeth against my neck in that dream I'd experienced after I drank the medicine that she had given me.

I told myself that it had just been a dream, because honestly…the alternative was too terrifying.

"Oh, come on now, sweet little siren, let me help you," she cooed in a breathy voice. Although intended to be sexy, the tone had the opposite effect on me. It didn't help that her left eye was twitching a bit as she talked.

I managed to hop off the sickbed, surprising myself once again by just how good I felt. How long had I been out? How long had I been left unattended with this crazy lady? I shivered just thinking about all she could have done when I was passed out and helpless.

Dr. Brina pouted as she lowered her scalpel. "You're no fun." Her eyes brightened as she thought of something. She dashed over to a few shelves covered in small bottles and pulled out a small clear vial filled with a light blue liquid. She looked over at me and began to approach, holding out the bottle for me to take. "Here you go. This will take care of that cracked rib issue you have going on, although I'm sad to say the rest of you is almost all the way healed."

"You're sad to say—" I began, before closing my mouth when a wicked smile splashed across her face, and she sliced the scalpel in front of my face, barely missing nicking my nose.

"You were saying, little siren?" she asked with a manic laugh. I had no intention of putting anything she gave me in my mouth, but I wasn't about to say that to her. I wanted to keep my nose, thank you very much.

I backed away from her as she continued to laugh, not looking away until I was out of her office and safely down the hall. I was dressed in what amounted to the gowns you always wore in the hospital, except whoever had undressed me had thankfully left me in my bra and underwear, so I wasn't flashing anyone as

I walked down the hall to where I thought my cell was.

This place was funny like that. You would think that you had gotten the general layout, and then it would be different the next day. Especially if I ever found myself without a guard, like I did now.

Suddenly, I felt a burn on my hand and yelped as I dropped the vial that Dr. Brina had given me onto the dirty, stone ground. Surprisingly, it didn't break.

I stared at it cautiously, wondering if I should just leave it there. I swore I could still hear her laughter echoing down the hallway though, and I did not want to chance her finding it and knowing that I'd just left it. I bent down, holding my gown closed behind me, and used the bottom of my gown to grab the vial. Using the cloth of the gown at least made it manageable to carry.

Not wanting to be caught in such a compromising outfit, I kept hurrying down the halls until I finally found my cell. Slamming the cell door shut behind me, I breathed a sigh of relief, wondering at how bad life was that I could feel a modicum of safety in my cell.

I stared at the bottle in my hand, and the blue liquid now seemed to be glowing. For some reason, I couldn't get myself to pour it down the toilet like I know I should. Instead, I stuffed it under my mattress, figuring I could ask Alaric about it later.

That decided, I laid back on the cot gratefully, my mind whirling with what all had happened. Was Seth alright? He had to be. I couldn't accept any other alternative.

My fingers brushed against my lips, thinking about that kiss.

That beautiful, perfect kiss that I wanted to repeat over and over again for as long as we both lived.

I sighed, a desolate tear slipping down my face as the image of his skin shredding on his back filled my mind.

I shouldn't have had that kiss with him. With Alaric and Keon, it was different. They were like me—damaged in a way that was insurmountable. Seth was the opposite. He was damaged, yes, but I could feel the purity of his soul every time I was around him.

What had happened to him was proof that I was poison and would only bring him down further.

Now the question remained—was I selfless enough to let him go?

I was ashamed that I didn't know the answer to that question.

CHAPTER 9

SELENA

My days in Nightmare Penitentiary were growing more intense by the moment.

Life in a prison was meant to be anything but complicated. When we were not confined to our cell, we ate and made the day pass by. But somehow, my stay here had morphed into a tornado of anxiety and emotions…and my heart already beat so hard at how fast things were moving between me and the three men who'd swept into my life.

I sat on the side of my bed, staring at the stark blank wall in front of me, but I was a million miles away. I drowned in so much that had happened. Fights. Seductive dinners. Horrific beatings. Everything was too much, yet I was so deeply ingrained in all of it, I didn't have a clue about how to pull myself out.

I couldn't even remember when it got to this point, but getting out seemed impossible. Well, the prison part was obvious, but finding myself attracted to three men, each so different to one another that if I was ever asked to choose between them, I'd laugh because it wasn't possible.

How did one choose between breathing and eating? I snorted a laugh under my breath as I thought back to how crazy addicted I felt toward Alaric after his fight, how intoxicated Keon made me feel in his arms, how my heart had broken and patched back up after Seth kissed me.

I'd gotten myself into a massive mess.

I wanted all three men as mine, but would they feel alright with sharing me?

Up on my feet, I pushed those thoughts aside, unable to think about such things, as they had my stomach clenching with anxiety.

I ran my hand through my hair, still damp from the fast wash I'd had this morning in the communal showers. The guard who was meant to take me to my shift said Seth was to have no visitors today. And when I begged him if he could let me out for a fast shower while other prisoners remained locked, he happily obliged. And it had nothing to do with him wanting to perv to my surprise. Nope, he wanted someone to listen to him talk non-stop about how hard his life was living in the basement to his parents' home, and well, I tuned out. I was in freaking prison, so if someone's life was hard, hello!

While chatting away, I did happen to catch him mentioning that the warden headed out of the penitentiary for a meeting. Ever since, my mind whirled around the idea of using this moment to fix a wrong.

To retrieve Seth's crystal.

It was my fault he got tortured additionally, and maybe if I returned it to him, he might tell me what was so special about the crystal. And what really happened with his father.

I glanced outside my cell through my open door where inmates sprawled across the hallway, leaving the cafeteria. Meaning the guards would be watching them and not question as I made my way toward the warden's office. I tapped my pocket where I had two hair pins. Maybe it was my luck to find them this morning in the shower room.

As I drew closer to the communal area, an open area connected by two hallways, I lowered my head and kept walking to avoid meeting anyone's gaze. The guard at the doorway didn't pay me attention, so I sped away.

Someone grabbed my arm from behind me, and I turned around to come face to face with Keon. My heart soared, and my smile instantly lifted.

"Hey, gorgeous," he whispered, bringing me so close we might be touching, but for the sake of others seeing us, he kept a sliver of a distance. My skin danced with goosebumps, remembering our recent time together.

I looked up into his green eyes, recalling the first time I stared into them at the bar. How I knew right then he was the guy for me. Maybe fate had brought us together, well aware we'd cross paths again. I liked to believe that was the case, though there was so much more about him I wanted to learn.

"I've missed you," I said. "Haven't seen you around for a few days."

He still held onto my hand, his thumb rubbing my inner wrist in gentle circles, and that small gesture threw me back to our last time together. To how incredibly insane he made me feel. Even days later, all those desires awakened inside me with renewed arousal. And my cheeks flushed as a tingle slid between my tights. I pressed them together, and it felt achingly incredible.

"Had a few days off work," he answered.

All I could think about was if he thought about me while he was out there in the world free. It occurred to me then just how little I knew about him. Maybe it was trusting of me, but I didn't believe he had a wife and kids he kept secret. When I had met him at the bar that first time, he seemed sure of himself and not a desperate, sleazy man. And it had been me after all who initiated the quick one-night stand.

The way he stared back at me then and again at this moment was of someone who knew what they wanted.

Me.

"I've forgotten what the outside world looks like." I laughed, even though that was kind of sad, to already feel like I'd been in this place so long.

"I will have to bring you photos of the city."

"And the outdoors," I said. "God, I miss walking

through parks and visiting the ocean. And the fresh smells."

His smile was infectious.

"So, what does a guard do on his time off?"

"Stay indoors, mostly," he answered, which I found odd. But when I thought back, I rarely left my home. A lot of that had to do with my controlling mother and Julian.

"I'm going to live vicariously through you, so you need to go places and then tell me how it was, okay?"

His mouth opened with his response, but it wasn't his voice I heard.

"Keon," another guard barked behind him. "Get over here."

Keon's face frowned, his brow pinching. "I'm on duty in the communal area, and I gotta go, but I'll see you soon." His hand slipped out of mine, and he turned, marching away.

With great effort, I didn't chase after him or beg me to take me to his room for time alone. But there was no stopping my gaze from dipping to his tight ass.

I had to find out more about who these men in my life were. Except that came later. Now, I pushed forward on fast legs and needed to focus on the mission at hand.

By the time I reached the cafeteria, there were still a few stragglers from breakfast. I scanned the room and spotted one of the food trolleys, and it had a platter with a few dirty plates, perfect. I frantically crossed the room and snatched the thing, then wheeled it out of there before anyone noticed.

Curved corridors took me left and right, past more cells and inmates and guards. It was only when I entered a passage with no one around and the sounds fading behind me, that my heart beat faster.

Running was out of the question, as that drew suspicion. At the end of the hall, I peered out into a brightly lit corridor with normal doors, not prison ones. This looked like the direction I'd used to reach the psychologist's office, so I stepped out and walked quickly left, pushing the trolley. A guard appeared from a doorway and marched toward me.

My heart slammed in my chest as he eyed me up and down. I kept my head down, but he stepped in my path. I hadn't seen him before, so chances were, he had no clue who I was either.

"What business do you have here?"

I looked up at him. "I've been given instructions to pick up dirty plates and clean up food in a meeting room."

He tilted his head to the side. "Who gave the instruction?"

My mouth dried with the lies. "My boss said it came from the warden." I shrugged. "I don't want to get in trouble, so I don't question my orders."

He scrutinized me for a long moment, and I made sure to pay attention to his badge name. John Welks.

He suddenly stiffened and tapped his earpiece, listening, then responded. "Fuck, how many? I'm on my way." The way he glanced back at me said he'd forgotten I stood there.

"The guard at the security pass around the corner will take down your details and accompany you to where you need to go." Without waiting for my response, he spun and darted down the hall, tapping his ear again. "Trevor, we need back up in Sector D, east wing. Now!"

Perfect timing, so I pushed my trolley until I reached barred doors and a guard inside a glass booth-like room off to the side.

He glanced up at me, sneering. "You're not permitted in here alone."

"John Welks confirmed I am to go through as I have to clean up the warden's meeting room before he returns."

When he said nothing but picked up the phone, I waited. I couldn't hear the conversation as he must have switched off the microphone, but he was nodding his head.

Sweat rolled down my back. Maybe I'd gone too far, and my own lie would end up being a noose around my neck.

Seconds later, the metal door slid open, and I pushed forward without asking another question. But several guards rushed past me and vanished the way I came. I had no idea what was going on back in the prison, but maybe it was a sign the universe was helping my cause.

When the tall, lofty guard with a crooked grin

stepped out of his booth, he said, "Follow me." He stormed down the narrow hallway with no windows or doors, and only our footsteps hitting concrete flooring resonated around us. The doors shut immediately behind us.

The guard fiddled with keys and opened up a door, then pushed it open. But his gaze was back on his booth, and that's when I spotted his badge. Christopher Smith.

"Go, and get this done quickly. Yell once you're done," he instructed.

I wasted no time and went inside as he rushed back to his post when his phone rang.

Inside, the meeting room had a round table, eight chairs, and not a mess in sight. The windows were barred, and when I went to look outside, I was greeted by a brick wall maybe a few feet away. Below, I couldn't see a thing.

I hurried back to the door and peered out, noting the guard was on the phone, his arm waving madly as he spoke, so I hoped that meant he wasn't accurately checking monitors either. I slid out of the room and darted in the opposite direction, knowing this was exactly where the warden's office lay.

My skin crawled at remembering his aggression, and he'd make my life hell if he found me. So I had to be fast—in and out.

Around the next bend, I swung left and didn't stop until I reached the huge black doors that lead into his office.

There were cameras around, the kind that swiveled across the hallway, so the moment it swung away, I tried the handle. Locked, of course. I grabbed the hair pins from my pocket and hastily leaned toward the handle, pushing them inside the lock, wiggling them. I'd never done this before, but watched movies and read enough to know this had to work.

I dropped my hands as the camera came away once again. Half a dozen tries, and still the door remained locked.

My arms shook, and now I was plastered in sweat, because someone was bound to have seen me standing here to raise suspicion. My saving grace had been whatever fight was happening back in the main prison section.

When someone cleared their throat behind me, I almost died. I couldn't move at first, and all I could picture was the warden standing over me, about to destroy my world.

I trembled ferociously as I took in a shaky breath and turned around with a bravery I didn't possess.

Brown eyes. That was what I saw first... The deepest, mud-colored eyes, and nothing looked familiar in them. Studying the round face, the short clipped hair, the ears sticking outward, it hit me quickly it was the same guard from the booth out front. Christopher.

"I-I'm--" My words flatlined, making me sound so suspicious. God, get it together. "I'm looking for the broom closet." That time, my voice steadied and I held his gaze.

His hand struck out, and he snatched my forearm, squeezing so hard I grimaced.

"You're with me," he growled, and hauled me down the hallway, past the passage that took me back to the meeting room and to a small hollowed alcove that seemed to be used for storage. He shoved me in there until my back slammed into the wall, and he towered over me, moving in closer…closer…closer.

Alarm bells exploded in my head, and the way he leered at me left my skin crawling.

"Get away from me," I snapped, and shoved my hand into his chest. He wasn't a big man, but he was tall and solid like most of the guards. I couldn't tell if he was of any supernatural kind, yet he kept me pinned in the corner.

"Why were you trying to break into the warden's office? He will make you hurt when he finds out. You'll be seeing a lot more of these walls, and he'll make every day a living hell. He has no mercy."

I swallowed hard, my entire body trembling, even if I kept telling myself he was trying to freak me out.

"You're mistaken," I explained, and lifted my chin high. "I dropped something and it slipped under the door, so I simply tried to see if I could retrieve it."

He barked a laugh in my face, sounding more like a hyena, and I loathed the way he studied me like I was the prey he was ready to tear apart.

"Listen, right now I have a video recording of everything you were doing." He reached over to push a strand of hair behind my ear, and I flinched against him. "Or I can easily go in there and delete the footage. Would you like that?"

I was too scared to answer, because everything about him reminded me of Julian. Everything he did required a payment. Men like them always took and stepped over everyone else.

"I'm not for sale," I retorted, and shoved to move past him.

But he moved too fast and grabbed me by the hair, shoving me back into place in front of him. He kept shaking, his eyes blinking too fast. Something was wrong with him.

"I can feel you inside me," he muttered. "It's playing with my head, and all I can think about is you." He stared at me with an infatuation I recognized from when my mother would use her power to captivate men with her power. Except my power shouldn't be affecting him this intensely while my power was suppressed in the prison. But that didn't stop my rational mind from yelling that I had to get away from this psycho.

Instinct kicked in, and I shoved my fists into his gut, but he gave no response, as though my hits were nothing.

Fear squeezed around my chest. "Get the fuck off me, before I scream."

"And then what? Your word against mine, when there is footage of you breaking the rules." He tsked at me, clicking his tongue, then shoved his face against mine.

A slobbery tongue poked out of his mouth and swept over my lips. Bile hit the back of my throat, and there was no stopping the sickness hurling forward. I spewed, and my meal came rushing out, right over the dickhead's chin and chest.

He jerked backward, screeching, his face twisting with disgust. "You fucking bitch," he shouted.

I wiped my mouth with my sleeve and shuffled sideways past him, my heart jackhammering against my chest.

He lashed out, and the back of his hand struck my face, the knuckles feeling like stone.

I stumbled backward and crashed into a wall, but hooray for me, I didn't fall over. My face flared up with a burning ache from where the bastard hit me. The pain pulsed, and it hurt so bad. But I took that moment to get out of there and darted back toward the hallway.

"You will pay for saying no to me. I'll make you my bitch, you wait and see!"

"Fuck you. You'll never touch me again." The power of a siren was double edged. Addiction and obsession were horrible traits that drove people to insanity. And I didn't have time to deal with his damaged mind.

I turned and sprinted away, but slammed into someone else around the corner. Bouncing backward, I cringed when I noticed it was John. The other guard I'd bumped into earlier.

"What's going on?" he barked.

"I just want to go back to my cell, please. Can you let me through?" I spoke quickly and glanced over my shoulder to where Christopher, the dickhead guard sneered.

"You alright?" he asked his friend. Of course he'd care about that asshole instead of me.

When Christopher simply nodded while giving me the death glare, John commanded, "Go clean yourself up, man." Then he looked at me with what I could only describe as a sliver of sympathy. Or maybe I was misinterpreting annoyance for understanding. "Let's get you back to where you belong."

I nodded and made sure to grab the trolley from the meeting room, while his words kept whirling around in my mind. Where I belonged.

This was how I was perceived. Not a person or a female or a siren…but just an object that needed to be put back into her box where I belonged.

My chest burned with those thoughts, just as much as it did that I'd failed to retrieve the crystal for Seth. Worst yet, now I had to worry about the guard reporting me to the warden.

CHAPTER 10

KEON

Not much changed in this joint.

Chaos broke out in the communal area over a goddamn card game. Give the inmates any reason to battle, and we'd have a world war within these walls. Not that I cared, because if it was up to me, I'd let them all tear each other apart. Well, nearly all… Not my sweet Selena. She was different and didn't belong here. So that meant protecting her with everything.

She was mine, I knew it from the first time I met her in the bar. From the moment I fucked her, something inside me changed. And it had grown into an obsession… Now she played on my mind constantly, and my cock twitched just remembering her sugary scent and taste.

Fuck, she was going to be my undoing. I felt it in the damn stone in my chest that never beat for anyone before. That was why I knew Selena was special. Oh so fucking special.

Security had swept in and taken the inmates who were fighting into maximum security, while most returned to normal after their daily entertainment had ended.

Now, I searched for Selena, weaving past inmates standing around and made my way to her cell.

Just then, I spotted her running toward her cell, her face ashen, head low, and if I'd ever seen someone running with fear, that was it.

I quickened my pace, my pulse spiking, and I stepped into her cell behind her.

"Angel, is everything alright?"

She spun toward me, surprised by my presence. Her eyes were glazed over while the side of her face blushed with a bright bruise forming just under an eye.

"What the hell happened?" I cupped her face, studying her trembling chin and the dread behind those beautiful eyes.

"I think I fucked up." Her voice held strong, despite looking like she might cry. But she kept herself together, and I was so proud of her for not falling apart.

"Tell me what happened."

She hesitated at first, but I drew her closer so she knew she could tell me anything and she'd be safe. Whoever the fuck touched would wish they were never born. But that wasn't something she needed to know.

"I was trying to break into the warden's office since

he's away, and someone caught me." She licked her dry lips and glanced down at her feet.

"Then what happened, Selena?" I didn't care that she wanted to break the rules and probably try to collect her orb from the warden. All I worried about was making sure she stayed safe.

"The guard who found me threatened to show the footage of me breaking into the office if I didn't sleep with him. Then, I kinda of threw up on him and he hit me." She grimaced when she met my gaze. "I don't want to stay in here forever."

White lights popped behind my eyes as fury rose through me like a tidal wave, crashing into me, ripping everything away.

Sheer anger trumped every other emotion. "Which guard?" I growled.

My little angel blinked up at me, and I saw the resistance on her face, not wanting to tell me at first.

"Babe, if you want me to fix this, I need a name."

She gave a small nod. "Christopher."

I ground my back teeth, as I'd always hated that douche after hearing he forced himself on inmates, then hurt them, leaving them broken, and sometimes, beaten severely. I'd always told myself other people's shit wasn't my business, and the scum in this place deserved punishment. Except, when it comes to Selena, everything changes.

A dominance blazed over me for her, and I trembled with pure rage seething within me.

"Stay here," I instructed her. "You'll be safe. I'll return later." Today was a good day for payback.

She grasped my arm. "Please don't get in trouble for me."

"Oh, Selena, for you, I would bring the world to its knees."

I adored the way she looked at me when I said that, her admiration awakening my own inner beast. And it drove my pulse and an unstoppable need to make Christopher suffer in a way that he would never forget.

I watched her sit on her bed, hands in her lap, and my heart shattered to see her in pain. I whipped out of the room like a raging storm. Every step slapped the ground, and people darted out of my way.

By the time I left behind the prison sector and found Christopher wasn't in the booth room, I kept going and searched all his usual hang out areas, including the kitchen and sleeping quarters offered to guards who worked two shifts in a row. Even the empty rooms I'd heard he took his victims. Nothing.

But when I stepped into the bathroom, I found him leaning over the sink, cleaning his guard's uniform with a wet paper towel.

I scanned the room. The doors to the toilet cubicles and two showers lay open. We were alone, so I shut the door and locked it from the inside. There were no cameras here, and I smiled to myself as I stepped deeper inside. The clock on the wall stated it was exactly one-thirty p.m.

Christopher's head jerked in my direction, his

upper lips curled into a snarl. "What the fuck are you looking at?"

"What happened to you?" I kept my voice steady, though my hands already curled tight.

"Some bitch, that's what happened. I'm going to fuck her up royally."

Holding back was useless because I only saw red, and I stormed across the room toward him like a wolf.

He jerked backward from me. "Whoa, man, what the fuck!"

I grabbed him by the throat and shoved him back up against the wall. "YOU fucked up! Selena is mine! And you laid a hand on her, you piece of shit."

"Get the fuck away from me," he spat, throwing a fist at my face in the same breath.

I felt nothing but the burning rage consuming me. A growl rumbled in my chest, and while I always fought to hold back the monster inside me, this time, I threw open the flood gates.

Christopher's expression was like granite, not showing a thread of fear, but then again, psychopaths rarely had emotions to show.

My skin pricked with the oncoming change... lashing over my body like barbed wire. A screeching growl tore past my throat, and I stumbled back, releasing Christopher.

He held himself still, staring at me with gaping huge eyes, and there it was, the trickle of fear I'd been waiting on. I smell it on him like perspiration. So I wasted no time, and quickly unbuttoned my uniform shirt, removing it along with my pants, shoes, and socks, and placed them on the bench at the back of the room and as far from the action as possible.

"The fuck, man, I'm not into dudes. You touch me with that dick, and I'll fuck you up," Christopher threatened. Oh, if only that was the least of his problems.

A shudder rolled through me as my monster pushed forward, faster and faster, while I slid back into the recesses of my mind. He loved to take over, and I'd been keeping him on a damn tight leash lately.

Time to play.

The change struck me instantly, and with it came the feeling of fire scorching every inch of me. When I opened my mouth, wisps of black smoke curled upward.

Christopher flinched backward. "You're a fucking demon! The fuck! Your kind is illegal to work here."

I shrugged, a huge belch spilling from my mouth, throwing out more smoke. A took a fast glance over to the mirror to my right for a split second to admire just how glorious this form was. Sure, it was forced upon me when I stupidly made a deal with the devil at a crossroad, but I'd embraced who I was long ago.

Black horns arched back from my temples, my eyes black as an onyx stone, and fangs sitting over my lower lip. I stood on all four, but my hands were clawed, my feet hooves.

A tremendous roar surged through me, and I was shoved back into my mind, the beast taking over.

Then everything moved at lightning speed.

Christopher ducked to run past me, but the beast snatched him by the top and shoved him into a shower cubicle. The guy cried out as he fell over his feet and hit the ground hard.

He stood no chance, and my beast lunged at him.

Tearing.

Slurping.

Scratching.

Screams… Oh so many glorious screams filled my ears. My vision blurred, taking me with it.

Arms and legs and teeth, Christopher fought, the poor sucker. They were the last things I saw before my beast took me over completely.

* * *

I flipped open my eyes to the bathroom ceiling. I exhaled, and a puff of black smoke expelled, emptying from my lungs. The last remnants of the demonic beast I'd lived with for years faded away, having sated himself.

Shoving myself to my ass, I sat in the middle of the bathroom, my hands bloody, and a metallic tang coating my tongue. I'd gotten used to the taste of blood, even if it left my teeth feeling furry.

I glanced up at the clock on the wall.

One-fifty p.m.

The bastard inside me didn't waste time. Then again, I had starved him for weeks.

Up on my feet, I stepped toward the shower cubicle that was splashed in blood and Christopher's body crumbled in the corner. I raised a brow. Maybe I should have given the beast instructions not to kill him.

Well, too late for that. And looking down at myself, standing only in my jocks, I thanked fuck I removed my clothes.

I threw myself into the cubicle to get this mess cleaned before someone crashed in here.

This bathroom held cleaning equipment in here, and bleach did wonders to clean up blood.

Cleaning up in record time, I finally lifted Christopher and shoved him into the trolley bin by the door. It was big enough for two grown men to hide inside in truth, and reached my waist in height. So it made for the perfect spot to conceal a dead body temporarily. I removed my underwear and threw them in there too. Leaning in, I covered the whole mess with towels.

Breathing easier, I turned to the bathroom and mopped up any blood I'd missed. Most of it had been contained to the shower, which I'd cleaned spotless. Then I jumped in and washed myself furiously of the last bits of blood. Red swirled into the drain, just like that fucker's life. I felt nothing for taking him out. Scum like him didn't deserve to keep breathing, as he'd hurt so many women, leaving them broken beyond repair.

By the time I dried off and got dressed, I looked at myself in the mirror and ran my fingers through wet hair. No sign of my horns, and the blackness in my eyes was almost gone. I looked as normal as any guy in this hellhole.

Exhaling loudly, I squared my shoulders. This wasn't what I wanted to do at work, but sometimes shit had to be taken out with the garbage. And when I looked over to the dirty towel bin that sat on wheels, I knew I'd have to find a way to get rid of it before anyone stumbled across it.

I stepped into my boots and made my way to the door where I unlocked it. I stepped out just as John, another guard was about to walk inside.

"Watch it," he snarled.

I opened the door for him and let him pass.

"Hell, why does it stink in here?" he gagged.

"Sorry," I called out. "The curry from last night isn't sitting well." The distinct stench of sulphur sometimes lingered behind when my beast made an appearance.

"Hell, that is filthy!"

I walked out and paused around the next corner, readjusting the phone piece in my ear, figuring I'd have to work out the best time to take out the trash.

A crackling came into my ear. "Keon, where the hell are you? You're on duty down in the yard. Fuck, man!" a new guard on duty snarled in my ear, and I gritted my teeth, glancing back to the bathroom.

I tapped the piece in my ear. "Hold your fucking horses. I've got to help out in the booth room. Be there soon."

As much as my gut clenched, I stormed out of there,

making a small detour to the booth first to delete some footage.

Covering your tracks after a murder is never easy.

Selena

"You ready?" Trevor started saying from my cell door.

I narrowed my gaze at him. "Ready for what?"

"Your regular psychiatrist trip." He stared at me like I was indeed crazy and in need of such counselling help. Maybe he was right, because this place did things to you.

Since Keon left, I hadn't been able to do anything else but worry. I was in enough trouble, and it would destroy me if he got in shit because of me.

"Let's go, pumpkin," he stated.

"Don't call me that," I answered. Last thing I needed was another crazy guy with complicated things. And then to have Keon go after him too.

I'd never had a guy fight for me, and yet both Alaric and Keon had now done that for me within days. Now, where were these men before I joined prison so they could've perhaps sorted out Julian? When I think back to Alaric saying he was the warlord leader of the southern territories, if there was anyone who could stand up to Julian, it would be someone like him.

Except, was even he powerful enough against the force behind Julian?

Up on my feet, I pushed those thoughts aside and followed Trevor along the hallways. I kept my head low and kept going over recent events, torn between the crazy and the most alluring men I'd met.

Why couldn't things just be about me meeting these men, end of no story. No psycho guards, no snake shifters, no accidentally giving away a fae's crystal.

We come to a stop outside Dr. Maynard's office, the prison psychiatrist. Apparently, to ensure inmates remained sound of the mind, we met with the doctor, but in all honesty, I questioned who exactly was the one needing the mental checking. There was something dangerous about Dr. Maynard. The way she looked at you felt like she reached down into your soul and yanked it out through your chest.

A halo of cigarette smoke surrounded her as she lounged in her leather seat, the room ripe with the smell.

"Hello, Selena." She rose to her feet with such ease that I could have sworn she was floating.

The guard left us behind and shut the door.

"How have you been?" she asked, walking out from around her desk. "Anymore strange dreams?"

I shook my head. "I've been sleeping like a baby. Once my head hits the pillow, I'm gone." Most of that had to do with so much happening during the day, that exhaustion claims me once night hits.

"That's great," she responded. Today, she was

wearing a tight pencil skirt the color of midnight that fell to just below her knees. Her white blouse was pulled taut across her chest, and her heels clicked as she crossed the room from the desk to the chaise lounge. "And have you managed to make any friends?"

I half laughed. "You make it sound like this is a friendly place. Half the time, I'm watching my back."

She gifted me with a lopsided grin. "Sometimes, you'll find the most unusual friends in the harshest of places, so maybe I can arrange for some group activities with other inmates that might be suited as your friend? Also, I have heard that you spent a bit of time with Seth."

"That's not quite friendship when I'm being forced to help him out." Her bringing up Seth made me wonder if the warden had instructed the doctor to pry information from me on Seth. The idea of being grouped with anyone sounded awful.

"Come, lie down for me."

I took fast steps forward and lay down, lifting my feet up, and now, I felt like I really was in a shrink's office.

She turned toward her glass cabinet against the wall, fiddling with glass vials. "I've been experimenting with something to help calm down the anxiety of my patients. I tried it with three others, and slowly over time, they found it easier to settle into the penitentiary."

Her words raised alarms, and I stiffened. "Oh, I don't need anything. I've made a few friends, and I am more than fitting in." My nervous words came out fast, tripping over one another.

"You do need to be selective, Selena, on who you choose are friends too. I would like to warn you against spending too much time with Alaric." She turned to me, holding a long glass tube with a circular end that reminded me of a pipe for smoking weed. "His background..." She licked her lips. "Is dangerous. Considering who you will be returning to once your time here is done, he is most likely not the best company for you."

I eyed her suspiciously, understanding exactly what she was saying in her cryptic explanation. Julian owned me, and me spending time with Alaric meant I conspired with the enemy. For all I knew, Dr. Maynard could be feeding information to Julian, so I had to remain on watch about what I said. And sometimes, that meant keeping my mouth shut.

She approached me, and my gaze never left the bong-looking device in her hands. It had a cork lid, and inside, gray smoke swirled around, trapped in there.

"I prefer not to try that," I explained. "I don't remember signing any waiver to be experimented on either."

She smiled, the thin lines around her eyes deepening. "There is nothing to worry about. This is just something to help relax your anxiety."

I shuffled to the edge of the lounge. "I'm not anxious. Why would I be anxious?" My voice seemed to squeak.

Before I could react, she popped open the cork, leaning the opening of the cylinder in my direction.

A puff of smoke gushed out and right at me. I coughed and waved a hand across my face to blow away whatever she'd just subjected to me.

Who in the world did this to her clients?

"Breath it in deep," she said, doing the same as if getting off on the smell.

I held my breath, refusing to inhale that stuff.

A strange tingling started at the base of my throat, and my eyes stung slightly. I swallowed several times to get rid of the feeling.

A breath expelled from my mouth. "What have you done to me?"

I went to move, but a heaviness pressed on top of me, while the edges of my eyes feathered with darkness.

Panic clawed through me, and I pushed to get up.

She reached down, placing a hand on my shoulder. "Rest, Selena." And as if her words carried the power of influence, I collapsed back down on the couch and my world darkened.

What felt like moments later, I opened my eyes and stared down. I floated up in the air, while my body lay crashed out in the lounge. What the hell?

The doctor returned to her desk, whistling to herself. I frantically glanced at myself.

I studied my hands. Pale and slightly transparent.

What the fuck! Had I turned into a ghost? Did she kill me?

I lowered myself and saw my chest rising and falling with each breath. Okay, I wasn't dead. Suddenly, I was flying through the room with a single thought. My legs kicked out of instinct as though I swam. I was having an outer body experience! Was this what the doctor had in mind when she said I would relax? Well, she was freaking wrong, because my heart was pounding insanely inside my chest.

I glided through the air on my stomach toward her desk, where she opened her laptop and started tapping away. When I shifted to hover behind her shoulder, I watched her open a new file and title it 'Experiment #5. Siren.'

Bitch. She had no permission to do this. But I wondered if she knew the impact of her concoction caused an outer body experience? She had inhaled the smoke as well, but hadn't passed out. I guessed whatever she created was made specifically for me—a siren.

When her phone rang and she answered, she started laughing and reclined in her seat. I figured she'd be a while. So I pushed toward the door to see about exploring. But I was moving too fast, and in my panic that I'd crash into the door, I jutted my hands out. Except they slid right through the wood and my whole body followed through it too. I caught a glimpse of the layered wooden panels of the door, then I was out in the corridor.

Excitement bubbled in my chest that somehow, I'd gained such freedom. I wasn't a fool to think this was long lived or offered me a way to escape, since my physical body was stuck back in the office. But I'd take freedom in any form it came.

And spying on everyone's business sounded perfect. My first point of call would be the three men who'd waltzed into my life.

What were they doing when no one watched? As crazy as it sounded, an excited buzz wormed through my stomach, like I might uncover a treasure on my hunt. Which made me think…if ghosts existed, was this how they felt most of the time? High on adrenaline while they spied on others, well aware there was no way they could get caught?

I flew down the hall and through walls with ease, passing over the heads of inmates and guards, most just milling around. I found myself up in Seth's quarter of the prison first, and when I slipped into his room, I half expected him to be lying in his bed. Except, he was sitting on the floor, the bedside table shoved aside, and he was leaned over.

Sliding alongside him for a better view, I paused as he expertly drew an image of my face and shoulders with a small piece of white chalk. He carefully made every stroke, studying his masterpiece, then adjusted the shading over my lips. The image was spectacular, so perfect and accurate, down to my slightly wonky eyebrow over my left eye.

There was something so beautiful and peaceful about watching him work. It seemed as though the process took him away from reality, and he was in a different world, escaping. He kept working on my hair meticulously, and my heart melted to see that he'd lost himself so much in picturing me. Had I really impacted him so much? Seth had been on my mind since I'd first crossed paths with him. Now, whatever was blossoming between us left me confused about where it would end. How could it go anywhere if he was here for who knew how long? Or was it until the warden killed him with the punishments?

Tenderness squeezed my heart, and I reached out to him. My hand passed right through his shoulder.

He stiffened and looked up in my direction. His eyes were glazed over.

Did he see me?

Except he seemed to stare right through me before returning to his artwork.

I retreated from the room, leaving him behind, and kept thinking there had to be a way for me to get the crystal back from the warden for Seth. It was the least I could do. Maybe on my rounds as a ghost, I'd pay the warden a visit too.

Once I reached Alaric's cell, I slid through the shut door, then froze mid-flight, my mouth gaping open.

My warlord was lying on his back in bed, his hand palming his huge cock, pumping his thick flesh up and down. His eyes remained shut, as he was miles away. Of course he'd be jerking off.

I hovered over him, unable to get myself to leave. Not when I devoured the sight of his strokes quickening, and all I could picture was me riding him rodeo style. My body hummed with a growing arousal.

Suddenly, he groaned, his chest arching, and his hand stiffened as ropes of cum spewed from his cock. God, the sounds he made… He moaned, his body rocking, and he was so fucking sexy.

When he opened his eyes and inspected his mess, he sighed. I left him to his cleaning and exited, then skirted around the corridor. I kept searching for Keon. Heading toward the office section, I decided to make my way to the warden's office instead.

The place seemed quiet, so I flew quickly.

Movement caught my attention from the corner of my eye.

Keon, darting into a room, taking a quick look over his shoulder before vanishing inside. His expression belonged to someone hiding a secret, so I followed him into the bathroom room.

He was half leaning into a towel bin, rummaging around, and I moved closer to look inside.

Just then, he uncovered a head.

I screamed at first, because that wasn't what I expected.

Keon kept looking over his shoulder at the door, while my gaze was glued on the dead person. And the more I looked at the guy with blood over his chin and mouth, the more I recognized him.

Christopher. The asshole guard who hurt me.

Oh, crap!

Keon killed the guard? I mean, I thought he was going to rough him up and threaten him. Not murder him! I sat on those thoughts for a few moments. It should have scared me, but I cared more about making sure Keon didn't get caught because he did this for me. The guilt of what I did to Seth burned through me as it was, I didn't want to feel even worse if Keon was sentenced to life imprisonment for me.

Christopher was a dickhead, and the only reason Keon would have killed him was if he deserved it. Did they get into a fight and things went bad? Whatever happened, Keon protected himself and me.

Footsteps sounded outside the bathroom. Keon frantically covered the body and sprinted into a toilet cubicle, shutting the door. And in that exact moment, my vision blurred.

The bathroom was ripped away from me, replaced with darkness.

What felt like seconds later, I opened my eyes to a pristine white ceiling and the smell of cigarette smoke. I'd returned back into my body.

I blinked and twisted my head toward Dr. Maynard's desk. No sign of her. The door was shut too. She'd left me alone, but would probably be back soon enough. My heart beat rapidly after what I just experienced. I thought it was all real and not in my mind. It seemed so real... Had Keon really killed Christopher?

Pushing myself up, my head swam at first, the room tilting. I patted my arms and legs, and I was definitely back in my body. Whatever she had given me was crazy and effective. Maybe not in the way she intended, but I might need to get my hands on more for future use if everything I just experienced was real. Guess there was only way to uncover the truth.

I sat there for a few moments, letting myself feel normal because my hands and feet still tingled like when I sit on them and lose all feeling.

The three men I attracted to my life were so different. One was talented and broken. The other a warlord with major sex addiction desires. And the third might have just murdered someone.

Yep, I had the perfect little harem of men, and it didn't matter if others saw them as monsters. Because they were my monsters.

Up on my feet, I stretched my back and hurried across the room, wanting to get out of there before the shrink returned and asked me a million questions. I had to go find Keon. This office didn't sit too far from where I'd seen him in my out of body experience. And if I had imagined it all, then I still got to see Keon, which definitely came with benefits.

Outside the office, there were no guards posted, so I took advantage of the moment and darted down the corridor.

Left and right, I took the turns, starting to slowly become familiar with the layout. Sweat broke across my brow the faster I traveled, but I didn't want to miss Keon and find out if what I'd seen had been real or not.

I approached a corner, and peered out. The passage to my right would eventually take me to the warden's office. I recognized the old painting on the wall in a simple black frame of a mountain range. With no real windows in this penitentiary, paintings were the next best thing.

Taking the left turn, I kept my head low and walked fast, hoping the guards on the security cameras didn't send someone out for me.

From my vision, the hallway looked like this one, with the flickering overhead fluorescent lights and the yellow stripes on the linoleum. I careened down the first left turn, which was a dead end. Nope, that wasn't the bathroom. The next passage proved a waste too, and I started to wonder if I had imagined the whole thing, when movement caught my attention from up ahead.

Keon pushed a towel bin into the corridor when he looked my way and our gazes locked. He froze, his eyebrows bunched up.

I darted toward him.

"What are you doing here?" he hissed through clenched teeth.

"Had a session with the shrink, and there were no guards waiting for me. Actually, I came to find you."

His attention kept bouncing from me to the corridor on either side of him. "Babe, this isn't the best time. You think you can make your way back on your own?"

I leaned in closer to him, pressing myself to his side. "Maybe I can help you?"

He studied me quizzically.

"Look, I know what's in the bin." I eyed the towel bin and then looked up at Keon.

His face turned a shade lighter. "No you don't," he growled under his breath.

"It's Christopher, now what is your plan?"

He stiffened and hastily hauled the trolley bin back down the small corridor leading to the bathroom, his other hand on mine, dragging me with him.

"How, do you know, Selena?" The fear in his voice deepened. "What haven't you been telling me?"

"The shrink blew some magic smoke in my face, and next thing I knew, I was having an out of body experience."

"And you came to check me out?"

I smirked sheepishly. "Of course."

He cupped the side of my face. I leaned against his touch, my insides fluttering with an explosion of butterflies beating their wings rapidly.

"So, what's your plan?" I asked.

"Take this out to the back dock where they have dumpster bins and toss out the rubbish."

"Why not take it to the inferno down in the basement? I had gone there once with a bunch of rubbish, and I just threw it straight into the fire. No evidence left. A guard escorted me." I winked, and I even scared myself at how easily disposing of a body came to me.

"You're not freaking out by this?" he asked with surprise in his voice.

"You defended yourself against the asshole, I get it. And you were defending my honor."

The way he stared at me felt like he wanted to say more, but shivers were crawling up the back of my legs as we remained there whispering near a dead body. Anyone could stumble on us and ask too many questions.

"We'll talk later, okay. Let's get this done," I said.

He drew me closer, and our mouths clashed for a split second. It was all I needed for my heart to race and remember why I fell so fast, head over heels for Keon.

Without another moment to waste, I took hold of the handle of the trolley bin and pushed it out into the main corridor, Keon at my back. We moved fast without a word. The two guards we passed didn't pay attention to me but exchanged greetings with Keon.

Coming to a stop in front of the elevator, Keon hit the button, and I chewed on my lower lip. Shivers slithered up my spine as we stood still and waited. I kept glancing down the corridor, expecting someone to come running up and accuse us of murder.

The ding finally sounded, and I flinched. Why the hell was I suddenly so nervous?

"Keon," someone yelled behind us.

I hurriedly pushed the bin into the huge metal elevator and turned around to find him talking to a female guard. Her mousey brown hair was pulled into a bun. She had the longest lashes and pale green eyes, and when she looked at me, they narrowed. God, did she know what we were doing?

Keon kept a hand on the doors, holding them open. "What's up, Joy?"

She batted her eyes when she turned to Keon. "Are you still up for swapping shifts next week?"

"Told you I was," he grumbled, getting into the elevator, and hit the only button to the basement while Joy stood there watching the doors close.

At the last second, she stuck her hand out to stop the doors from closing.

"What's going on, anyway? Since when are you escorting an inmate to take the towels to the basement?" She studied me from head to toe, and I squirmed on the inside because my plan was flawed. They had cleaners for the office sector of the prison. Shit, shit, shit.

"Why are you giving me hell, Joy?" Keon groaned.

"You know why," she sneered.

The silence between them thickened to where it felt like I breathed through molasses.

Eventually, she stepped back and Keon jabbed his finger into the close button. The doors shut with a final thump.

"She likes you," I stated flatly. "She seems very stalk-erish. Want me to take her out?" I half smirked when he looked over to me, and he rewarded me with an air kiss.

"She's not on my radar. I have my sights locked on you, gorgeous."

I couldn't hold back the beaming smile at his compliment.

The lift shook, sending us into a stumble before the doors groaned open.

An oppressing heat slammed into me first, and even breathing hurt my nostrils. The last time I came here was for five minutes, and I'd never forget how dark and awful it was. The brick walls seemed to drip with perspiration from the heat, the lights dim, and there was only one way to go…a tunnel-like corridor that led straight to a door at the end to the furnace room.

"What's down here beside a furnace?" I asked as I pushed the bin out of the elevator.

"A prisoner."

I glanced at him with shock on my face. "Only one? What is he or she, a god?" I half chuckled, but Keon didn't find it funny. Fuck, was it a god?

The wheels of the trolley bin crunched on the ground that was earth, the whole thing bouncing about.

"When you say 'god,'" I began, but he interrupted me.

"It's more of an uncontrollable demonic wolf."

My mind spun with questions… So many of them.

Keon snorted a short laugh. "No, I'm not answering everything now. So don't ask." He knocked on the basement door.

Seconds later, it opened, and we were greeted with a guard.

The earlier worry slammed into me once again, and I lowered my gaze.

"Dirty shit doesn't go down here," the guy stated at the door, standing in our way. "Take it up to laundry."

"Wish it was that easy," Keon joked, hiding his

worry smoothly. The guy was good. "These here are blood stained by someone really sick, and I got orders to burn them. Come, I'll show you." He shifted over to the bin and leaned in.

"Fuck no, man. You keep that infection crap away from me." The guard stepped aside, and waved us inside a massive room. "Go, do it fast."

The heat curled around me, and I sweated profusely already. It felt like we walked into the furnace, instead of toward it directly ahead of us. The black walls and ceiling only made it hotter in here.

Several inmates were in the corner, flattening boxes from a mountain of them, their faces cherry red, their clothes spotted with sweat stains. Thank hell the warden hadn't sent me to work down here.

Keon collected the extended stick near the furnace that looked like a giant metal wood fire oven, and drew it open. The fire roared.

I cringed and squinted my eyes, covering them with my hands. The heat was insane, and I might not have any eyebrows left after this.

"Let's get moving," Keon barked at me so everyone heard.

Wiping the sweat from my upper lip, I dug into the bin and yanked out a towel, revealing a hand. My heart beat ridiculously at how we were going to do this.

I rolled up the towel and tossed in into the fire and backed away instantly from the blaze. There go all the hairs on my arms.

Keon stood next to me and whispered, "Go to the

guard and cause a commotion. Something to attract his attention and the inmates from me."

My stomach dropped through me. "Are you kidding. "I'm not good at doing that. What am I supposed to do? Flash them?"

"Hell no. Don't you dare flash them. You are for my eyes only. Now go, you'll think of something." He nudged me in my back, and I stumbled toward the guard.

Just great! I kept chewing on my lower lip, which tasted salty from sweat.

The guard's head jerked up on my approach, and I made sure to pivot when I faced him, so he turned his back to Keon.

"What do you want?" he asked.

It was so hot in here, I swore I would pass out. "Do you have any water down here?" I squeaked and clasped my throat. "I don't feel well." I went with that angle. But when he wasn't buying it, I made a strange half-moaning, half-gurgling sound, and dropped to my knees, then started crying out of pure panic.

The guard quickly crouched down with me, and I looked over my shoulder to see the inmates had stopped working and looked our way.

Keon better be dumping that body into the furnace.

"Come with me." The guard took my arm and hauled me to my feet then outside the room where the colder air made breathing bearable.

"It's cooler here." He turned to head back into the furnace room, but I grabbed his arm.

"Please, don't leave me. I'm scared."

I sounded so stupid, and I cringed hard on the inside. But the guy bought it and stayed by my side.

"What's your name, sweetheart?" he asked.

I moaned as though I was in too much pain to hear his question.

His hand rubbed my back, heading lower to my ass a bit too quickly. Sometimes, my allure was a damn curse.

"I just need some space," I insisted, and pushed against him.

But he wasn't backing away or releasing me.

Heavy footfalls sounded, and I ripped myself away from him as Keon approached. "Oh, geez, I am starting to feel so much better now."

Keon eyed me, and the guard looked ready to jump on me.

"Alright, man, thanks for that," Keon snapped, and pushed me toward the elevator.

By the time we were inside and the doors shut, I exhaled loudly. "Fuck that was close. Did you do it?"

"Sure did. And you were amazing. After that, I want to fuck you so badly." His voice dipped to a seductive tone, and as if my body responded to him, a blaze curled in the pit of my gut.

Once we emerged from the elevator, Keon paused, tapping the piece in his ear. He nodded, and I stared up at him as his face twisted with frustration. I guessed this meant we weren't celebrating.

"I'll be right over." He lowered his hand and looked over. "We'll have to postpone, angel."

"Of course." I held back the disappointment pouring through me.

"Something big is going down in the prison."

We moved with haste back to my cell where he left me, and then took off without even a kiss. Not sure why I expected it when we had to be careful with our relationship. And after everything that just happened, I needed time out for reality to really sink in.

Christopher was dead.

Joy suddenly sauntered into my cell, the female guard who had been trying to pick up Keon back at the elevator.

The hairs on my nape shifted that she so conveniently appeared here in my room.

"Did you follow me back here?" I asked.

But she didn't respond and closed the distance between us. "I've heard about you. The siren who's fucking our dear Keon." Her nose wrinkled with pure disgust.

"He's good in bed isn't he?" she continued. "But don't let him fool you. You are not the first prisoner he was obsessed with. Keon has a compulsive issue. You are not his first victim, and you won't be the last either."

It took me a moment to process her words that came rushing at me. "What are you talking about? Why are you telling me this? Did he reject you?"

She barked a laugh in my face. "Girl, you're so

blinded by him already, aren't you? I'm simply doing a good deed and warning you before it's too late for you." She dug into her pocket and pulled out what looked like folded newspaper pages. She opened them and showed me articles titled, "Stalker Claims Another Victim." The next one mentioned, "Stalker Released on Good Behavior." The next three articles were along the same vein. I quickly took one and scanned the article about how Keon had stalked a female in her home, visited her daily, broke into her house, and threatened to kill anyone who touched her.

My stomach twisted on itself. No, this couldn't be right…yet everything I knew of him fit this profile.

The way he was always around me.

His dominating nature.

He killed a freaking guard who hurt me.

Keon was a serial stalker.

The guard folded up her articles and stuffed them back into her pocket. "Just figured you should know what you're getting yourself into. This is the only job he's allowed to do, but it hasn't stopped him from stalking females in here."

I stumbled over to my bed and flopped down. I didn't hear the guard's last words as she slipped out of my cell. Instead, I curled up in bed and hugged my pillow as a sickness rose through me.

Did I even know who Keon really was? How long before he moved on to his next victim?

CHAPTER 11

ALARIC

I couldn't fucking believe I was doing this. This was going to infinitely complicate my life and my plans, but here I was, walking to the warden's fucking office to get the crystal for Selena.

Fuck my life.

One nasty side effect for a newly mated incubus was their desire to please their mate. I'd, unfortunately, began experiencing this side effect basically as soon as her mark had appeared on me. It was hard to get anything done when you were always forced to think about what could make someone happy. Seeing her face when I told her I wouldn't help her that first time had been a particularly unpleasant memory to relive, over and over again.

I'd finally had enough. So here I fucking was.

My plan was working perfectly thus far. I'd paid off a group of rat and honey badger shifters to cause havoc in three of the mess halls. They would create enough damage that most of the guards would be sent over to assist in the cleanup and recapture of the shifter prisoners. Those honey badger shifters in particular would keep them busy for a long time. I knew for a fact that they allowed themselves to be caught and sent here over and over again because of the fights it allowed them to get into while they were here.

Crazy little motherfuckers.

I'd also had some of the vampires and succubi released for the evening in some of the maximum-security units. Between the vampires trying to drain everyone dry, since they were basically starved here as the warden's favorite form of punishment, and the succubi causing the others to start trying to have sex with everything that moved, I'd be free and clear.

I regretted not being able to watch what I'd put in place. I always loved a good orgy.

I'd also ensured that Selena would be safe. Keon, the psycho, was watching over her tonight and making sure she didn't leave her cell.

All those ends tied up, I had been free to head to the warden's office. Hopefully, there were a few other things that I could take at the same time to make this worth it. I wasn't going to admit to myself that seeing my mate's face when I handed her the necklace was payment enough.

I stayed in the shadows as I walked. One of the treasures I'd found in this place was a sort of cloaking device. If there was any darkness around you, the device took the darkness and wrapped it around you so that you were invisible to everyone around. Of course, it wouldn't work very well in the light of day, but here in the prison where everything was dimly lit, it worked perfectly. And it helped me pass through the manned doorway heading toward the office section of the building as it opened to a ground of guards rushing out.

I strode around a corner, a little disappointed when I saw that the usual guards set up outside of the warden's office were also not around. Evidently, my plan was working a little too well. What was a good breaking and entering without a few cracked bones?

I rolled my shoulders back, summoning a good dose of lust just in case the warden was inside the office and not checking on the carnage I'd set in motion. The warden's office was usually bright. For a shadow demon, he sure did like the light. But maybe that was because he knew firsthand the dangers that lurked in the dark.

Using my skeleton key, I opened up the door and stepped inside. The office lay empty when I stepped through. I knew there was some kind of silent alarm that was most likely set off as soon as I'd come in. The warden wouldn't have left all of his treasures unattended after all, the greedy bastard. I needed to get in and get out before he came back if possible. Although, I was kind of hoping for the warden to come... That would make my next few weeks here even more exciting.

I was sure it had been a while since someone had

broken in, and he would be furious. He'd be in my dreams, trying to feed off my soul for weeks. I didn't mind though, the nightmares that haunted my dreams at night were far worse than anything he could do. Shadow demons fed off of the fear they elicited in your nightmares. But if your mind was already beyond fucked up, you had instant protection.

I guessed my past was good for some things.

I strode over to the bookshelf on the far wall where I was sure he would have placed the crystal. I'd noticed on my perusal of his treasures in previous visits when he'd called for favors from me that he kept his treasures categorized. This one in particular seemed to always hold his favorite things. These items usually became his favorite because of how much pain it caused its previous owner when the item was taken from them.

I imagined that the fae prince's precious amulet was one such thing.

I had to give the warden credit where credit was due. He was a particularly sadistic bastard. I could learn a thing or two from him to take back home.

As I glanced through the shelves to find the crystal, I also searched for anything that looked like Selena's power. Selena and I hadn't talked about it much. She probably figured that after I'd rejected her last request to steal something, the last thing I would do was help her steal something else.

So I wasn't sure exactly what I was looking for. Power was different for everyone. For example, I'd once sucked the power out of a poltergeist, and it had resembled a grey mist in the bottle. I was certain that Selena's power would present a much stronger form than that. But the warden could have been keeping it anywhere.

There. I'd finally found Seth's crystal, draped around the head of a Greek statue, like how human jewelry was displayed in their stores. Finding a few other interesting looking things, I continued to keep my eye out for anything that looked like it could be Selena's power. But I didn't see anything.

My eyes swept over a spot in the cabinet twice where it looked like the dust had been disturbed. There was a faint power residue left on the glass, suggesting that whatever had been there had been an object of great power.

Unfortunately, there was no way for me to know by the power residue what that object had been.

I spent the next ten minutes looking through the other shelves to see if he'd placed it anywhere else. I didn't find anything that looked right, and I didn't expect to. A siren's power would have definitely been something that would make it to his "most valuable" shelf. Even I got heady from the depth of Selena's power.

I tried his desk last, but the bastard had locked every drawer, and not with the simple kind of locks that could be easily picked. I narrowly missed getting hit in the face with some kind of green acid when I sprung a trap trying to get into one of the bottom drawers. I'm sure that I eventually could have managed to unlock all the drawers. But I didn't have the right tools with me or enough time currently... I was surprised that the warden hadn't made his way back already.

Cursing that I couldn't find Selena's power, I stepped back into the hallway, blending in to the shadows once again.

Not a minute passed before I saw the warden making his way down the hallway, looking extremely pissed off. "I'm going to kill him," he muttered as he stormed towards me. I stepped out of the way right before he would have hit me, and he stopped a few inches away, sniffing the air as his gaze darted around the hallway.

He growled, and my hackles rose, ready to fight if he suddenly decided to attack the shadows at random to try and find me.

"I know you're there, Alaric," he hissed. "And I'm not amused. If I find out you've taken something from me, I'm going to find a way to make your life hell. Don't think for a moment I don't know that you're behind today's events." His eyes continued to dart around suspiciously, trying to find me.

I decided to send out a dose of lust just to fuck with him, since the cloaking device was keeping me well encased in the shadows.

I had to hold my laugh in when the warden popped a boner and let out a roar that dislodged rocks from the walls. I narrowly missed being hit in the head by one of them. He stalked off to have a good jerk-off session, I was sure. He was just lucky I'd barely used my power on him. I heard a roar and knew that he'd discovered something was missing from his office.

Waiting to make sure he didn't appear to resume his search for me. I ambled along the hallway. The warden would try to find a way to come after me for the missing crystal, but he would try and be sneaky about it. I would have to have my guard up even more until I got out of here. Or maybe I could find him another trinket to satisfy him.

Yes, that would work.

Making a note to get a medusa head, I strode down the hallway towards Selena's cell.

Time to win some fucking brownie points.

* * *

Keon was leaning against the wall across from her Selena's cell, staring at her avidly. I'd caught him doing this quite often when I was passing by to check on her.

"Boo," I whispered in his ear a moment before I powered down my cloaking device and appeared next to him. I couldn't resist fucking with him. Keon jumped at least a foot in the air, his eyes temporarily turning so black, I couldn't see the whites of his eye. He let out a low growl when he saw it was me and turned back towards Selena.

"You can go now," I ordered. "I've got it from here."

Keon's fists clenched, and he snarled at me. The stark possessiveness in his face would have frightened a lesser being, but I just smirked.

"I'm sure they need all hands on deck for the bit of a mess I've created," I told him. Just as I said that, I could hear his earpiece turn on as someone barked at him to head over to where the rat and honey badger shifters were still causing mayhem.

"Whatever you did better not blow back on her," he warned me before shooting Selena one last longing look and stalking away. I rolled my eyes. Like I would ever let anything happen to my mate.

I'd been impressed that he'd been willing to help me, even with me not giving him any details as to what I would be doing. I guessed all it took to convince him was me telling him that I was getting something Selena had asked for. Pathetic fucker.

My hypocrisy was strong today.

Selena sighed in her sleep, and I forgot all about Keon. I opened her cell door and stepped inside, content to just watch her for a moment.

She was beautiful, the kind of beautiful you couldn't forget. The kind of beautiful that made you stay up all night, wondering how you could keep it in your life forever. The kind of beautiful I was never going to let go.

I finally started to feel a bit like a creeper just staring at her, so I walked over to her bed and sat down beside her, wincing at how uncomfortable it was. I was going to have to get my supplier to get her a better bed, pronto. While my bed looked like the trash that everyone else slept on, it was really one of the top-of-the-line mattresses that had me sleeping blissfully every night. There was nothing a little spell couldn't hide. Since my ass hit a spring every time I shifted on this thing, it was clear Selena definitely was in need of some help. I mentally cursed myself for not thinking of it before.

Selena muttered something in her sleep, her forehead wrinkling up as she dreamt about something that evidently was unpleasant. I gently stroked her cheek, and she immediately relaxed her face.

"Seth," she whispered softly, longing all over her face.

What the fuck.

Hell. No.

Selena

I woke up to Alaric on top of me, stretching me with his cock as he pushed inside me. Halfway in, he stopped, before pulling almost completely out. Then he plunged in hard and fast, slamming into me so deep that I felt like he'd become a part of me.

I gasped from the sensation. I wasn't sure why he was here, but I wasn't going to complain.

"There you go, my queen. There's my cock. Right where it belongs... Feel that?" he asked as he somehow pressed even further in, stretching me wide, filling me beyond capacity. I whimpered. "Feel my cock inside you? Feel how I own you?" His voice was thick and harsh as he looked down at me, his cock twitching and pulsing deep inside me. "I own this body."

His rough voice set me on fire. He pulled my hips towards him, trying to get further inside me. His splayed hand slid up in between my breasts, to my neck, pressing on it just enough to let me know he owned me. I was only faintly aware that he'd somehow gotten all my clothes off.

"Keep your eyes on me," he ordered. I couldn't have taken my eyes off him, even if I wanted to. His face was savage with lust. I was mesmerized by the pure need and hunger in his eyes, and stunned at how hard he was inside me.

"I'm going to fuck you hard and rough."

Everything in me tightened, a whimper escaping me as I pushed into him.

"You're gonna take it. You're gonna take all of it. Everything I have to give you. Because you know who owns you, don't you?" He let out a deep groan as he started fucking me. Long, hard strokes. All the way in, nearly all the way out, grunting with each impact. A shudder ran through me as his hand flexed on my neck, still applying pressure and holding me down. His stomach and chest tightened, clenching as he thrust into me. His hips pumped at a bruising pace as his other hand pulled my hip into him, hard and rough. My eyes closed reflexively, focusing on him inside me, brutally pounding into me, giving me that sweet pain.

"Keep your eyes open. Watch me," he ordered again, the muscles in his arm shifting and jumping as he applied pressure to my neck. "Watch me fuck you." My body clamped down on him once, responding to his harsh words. I watched his body tightening and straining with his movements. My eyes settled on his sculpted face. He looked determined and fierce. Almost feral. I was consumed by an overwhelming need to please him, to submit to him. I let my hands run along his hips, feeling the flexing muscles under my fingers. He pressed my neck down harder, pushing me further into the cot. I felt the dominance in his posture, in the way he held me down.

"Alaric," I murmured through panting breaths, my body relaxing underneath him.

"Yeah. That's it, my queen. Just let go. Let me take over," he grunted, fucking me deep and hard. His hips slapped against me, rubbing against my clit with each thrust.

"Alaric," I whimpered.

"Yeah. You like that, don't you? Me controlling you. Fucking you so perfectly that you're never going to forget me." He thrust brutally into me, sending my orgasm rushing toward me. "Tell me you love it."

"Yes. I do. I love it. I love the way you fuck me," I murmured.

"Come. Right. Now," he growled, fucking me even harder.

My insides pulsed and fluttered at his words. His grip tightened on my neck, his pounding hips jolting me backwards with each thrust, his cock battering into me. His voice turned hard and demanding as he ordered again, "Now."

"Yes," I moaned, my muscles clamping down on his cock over and over, pleasure pulsing violently through me, so much that I didn't think I could handle it.

"You. Are. Mine." His voice was gruff, his breathing harsh as he continued to move as if he was pounding the message into me.

"More," I cried as another climax built.

"It's yours. Whenever you want it. You fucking own it." He slammed into me with bruising force, again. His hand tightened painfully, holding me in place.

"Don't stop." My words were broken by my gasping breath.

"Yeah, you love my cock, don't you? You can't live without it, can you? Come for me again, my queen. Show me who owns you."

His hand reached down, finding my clit. I felt another surge of pleasure running through me, exploding in my core. My body bucked, my muscles squeezed tight, clamping down on him. His frenzied thrusts extended my orgasm. Then he pinched my clit hard. I didn't recognize my own voice as an animalistic groan tore from my throat, pleasure pumping through me painfully. "Selena. Yes. You're perfect."

His voice was both eager and desperate. Fuck…

"Alaric," I cried, riding out another intense climax. My body convulsed, my muscles gripped him tighter. I never wanted him to stop.

"Oh, fuck, yes. I love your body. I'll never get enough of you." He groaned as his rhythm faltered. He thrust deep, grinding into me as he came. He folded over me, covering my body with his own, his hands cupping my breasts, his arms wrapped around me. His panting breath heated the skin of my neck as his lips brushed back and forth, muttering something that sounded suspiciously like the word love as he took several long moments to recover.

My cot was small and Alaric was heavy, but I soaked up the feeling of having him all around me.

He sighed and buried his head in my neck for a moment before shifting so he was only halfway on me. I immediately missed him.

"Fuck. I'm sorry," he whispered gruffly, studying my face for something. I stared back at him, my heart hammering uncomfortably. I hated this feeling I got around all three of them. It made me feel weak to care for them this much. Anyone I'd ever cared for in the past had let me down.

What would make them any different?

"What are you sorry for?" I asked, realizing belatedly that I had no idea why he'd said that.

He dropped his forehead against my shoulder and groaned. "I just fucked you like an animal. You're going to have my marks all over your body after that."

"Somehow I don't think you're sorry about that part. But you don't need to apologize. I was surprised, but I loved every second of it. I love how wild and uninhibited you are," I admitted to him shyly. "It feels like you can't get enough of me."

"I can't get enough of you," he agreed, disgruntled, as if the idea that he needed me repulsed him.

"I'm not complaining," I whispered to him when he lifted his head again to meet my gaze. "What brought this on though? I'm always up for a little surprise cell sex…but…"

He shifted against me, and I could feel the tension coiled inside of him.

"Tell me," I ordered, pulling him towards me so I could feel his lips against mine once again. I was already ready for more. My body's reaction to him wasn't as alarming as it was in the beginning though. I was addicted to him. His mere presence had me lust drunk, it was hard to think straight. I just wanted more, more, more.

He pulled away from me, his pupils dilated so I could barely see the gorgeous grey.

"I came in here to give you a fucking present, and you were dreaming about that pathetic fae," he growled. "You make me crazy. I'm desperate for you. I just want to keep you forever. I want you to be mine. I need you to be mine." He reached up and grabbed my chin, applying light pressure to it as he brought me closer.

"I'm sorry for not controlling my dreams?" I told him sassily. He squeezed my chin tighter in response.

"Have you fucked him yet? Does he know what you feel like, what you taste like?"

I didn't say anything. I just stared at him defiantly.

"You haven't yet, have you? He doesn't deserve you."

"And you do?" I responded.

He groaned as if my words physically pained him. "None of us do. But I'm not going to give you up. You're mine now."

"Even when I'm also theirs?"

"That doesn't change anything," he said fiercely.

"I'm sorry that I was dreaming of him," I told him, this time meaning it. "If it makes you feel any better, it wasn't a good dream."

"It does," he responded, sounding infinitely more cheerful.

I rolled my eyes as he levied another hard, possessive kiss on my lips. "You were saying you brought me something?" I reminded him once he pulled away.

A haughty, proud look appeared on his too perfect face. I couldn't believe that this god-like creature was currently wrapped around my body like an anaconda. The fates were really looking out for me in the man-candy department.

I was naked, while he was still completely clothed besides his pants being slightly pulled down. I was reminded of this when he reached into his pocket and pulled out...Seth's crystal!

My mouth dropped open. "How did you...?"

"I should have gotten that for you when you first asked for it," he told me. "It just took a second for me to come to my senses."

"I can't believe you were able to steal this out of the warden's office." I was completely shocked. It was the last thing I'd ever expected for him to do. "I can't believe you would do that for him."

"I did that for you," he growled, his face looking murderous. "I'd do anything for you."

His vow was fierce, and the presence of the crystal in my hand was proof that he meant every word of that promise.

Slipping the crystal onto the ledge behind my cot, I grabbed the bottom of his shirt and started to inch it off his body.

Alaric definitely deserved a reward...

* * *

We were both breathless and satisfied after the second round. I'd never imagined that sex could be like this. I think I might have even worn out Alaric, an incubus. I was a little proud of myself about that.

"So word around the prison is that you've been spending a lot of time with the fae lately," Alaric said casually as he stroked my hair.

"A fair amount," I conceded as my thoughts drifted to that kiss...and all the torturous moments before that.

I turned around so that I was facing him. He raised an eyebrow at me in question. "He's actually a really amazing man," I told him hesitantly.

Something sparked in Alaric's gaze, something that looked a lot like jealousy. "Of course you'd be the one to think that the prince who killed his father for the crown was 'a really amazing man.'" He rolled his eyes, as if he couldn't believe how naïve I was.

I pushed back away from him, annoyed. "I can't imagine him doing something like that," I told him fiercely, surprising myself at how fervent I sounded in my belief in Seth.

He pushed my hair back away from his face. "I'm sorry, that came out wrong. I just wish you were spending more of that time with me. How have you been able to get away with so much time with him? It must be a lot if I'm hearing about it in my section. Doesn't delivering meals take up most of your day?"

I hesitated for a moment, not sure of how much to say. But this was Alaric. If he'd done anything by stealing the crystal back from the warden, it was earning my trust.

"The warden wants me to spend that much time with him. It's become my new 'job' so to speak," I explain haltingly. The rest of the story flows out of my lips. It's a relief to tell someone about it. Alaric listens avidly. His face is neutral though, I can't read what he's thinking at all.

"So he wants me to find out where the scepter is, but I'm not going to do it. I won't do it. I've already caused Seth enough pain, and I don't trust the warden at all," I finished.

"Do you think Seth even knows where the scepter is? I don't want you to have the warden coming after you before I can get us away because of a mission you can't even fulfill."

I thought about it. "I don't know. If he does, he certainly hasn't said anything. The warden has him tortured so much that he barely has the energy to talk to me at all. He's just trying to survive."

That same look was in Alaric's gaze. He really was jealous about this. I doubted he would be jealous if he'd watched Seth's skin be flayed off his back because of the warden's anger at me.

"Just be careful," Alaric said. "If Seth says anything about the scepter, come to me before you say anything to the warden. We can come up with a plan together of what to do."

"I'm never going to get used to not being alone anymore," I whispered to him as I snuggled into his chest.

"You'll never be alone again," he vowed.

At his proclamation I couldn't deny, I definitely fell a little bit more in love with him.

CHAPTER 12

SELENA

It was nearly impossible for me to contain the giddiness I was feeling as I walked rapidly towards the section of the prison where Seth's cell was located. I couldn't wait to see his face when I gave him back the crystal.

I patted my pocket for what felt like the millionth time, making sure it was still there. I was sure there were a lot of creatures in this prison that would want the crystal if given the chance.

Hopefully, Seth had a better hiding place for it than he did last time.

The smell of Seth's cell block hit me first. His area was the worst part of the prison that I'd seen, resembling something closer to a decrepit torture chamber during the French Revolution than anything in this century.

Slipping around the corner, I saw Seth sprawled out

on the ground, a pensive look on his face as he stared up at the ceiling.

"Hi," I whispered to him as a guard appeared to open the cell door. Seth stood up, his face alight with happiness. Most of his injuries had healed. It was a testament to the strength of his power that the only evidence of his torture the other day was the faint bruising on his face. I bet if he took off his shirt, his back would be almost healed as well.

"Selena." He said my name reverently, and a rush of pleasure spun down my spine at the sound of it.

I felt shy all of a sudden. Something had changed between the two of us from that kiss and our mutual torture session. Something big.

I smoothed a piece of hair behind my ear nervously. Summoning courage, I walked up to him and grabbed his hand. "I have something for you," I told him, biting my lip.

His gaze strayed to my lips, and I could see the yearning in their depths.

"Did you bring me a present? It's not even my birthday," he told me with a wink. My mouth actually dropped open at the lightness in his voice. Words that described Seth best included 'brooding' and 'angst-ridden.' I wouldn't have believed he was capable of joking if I hadn't heard it for myself.

A smile broke across my face. It was delayed because I was absorbing everything about the moment, but I couldn't not smile at seeing a glimpse of what seemed like the real Seth, before everything terrible had happened to him.

"My delivery must have been terrible, judging by the look on your face," he said with a wink, and my insides sparked up with a whole lot of lust. Which was surprising, since I was still aching from the rounds I'd just gone with Alaric.

My vagina had become quite the hussy since coming to prison.

A snort burst out of me at that thought, and Seth's smile brightened even further at the sound of it.

Shaking my head to try and clear it from the euphoria-induced fog I was experiencing, I pulled him closer to me.

Reaching into my pocket shakily, I pulled out the crystal and held it out to him, making sure to keep it shielded between us and out of sight of the always watching guards.

He looked down at it, his smile fading as he stared at the crystal like it was a mirage that had suddenly appeared in the desert.

"How did you..." he began, until his voice became too choked up to continue. He didn't immediately grab the crystal. He just continued to stare at it like he couldn't believe it was real.

I took his hand and gently placed the crystal into his trembling palm. He immediately closed his hand so he was clutching it tightly, his eyes closing at the same time as he struggled to control his emotions.

"I'm sorry that you were ever parted with it to begin with," I whispered, feeling very emotional myself.

"I never explained to you why this was so important to me, did I?" he finally said in a gravel filled voice still choked with emotion.

I shook my head, holding my breath in anticipation of what he was going to say.

"When a royal fae passes into the next life, they leave a part of themselves in a crystal taken from the Othenian caves of the Light Realm."

"Leave a part of themselves?" I asked, not understanding what that meant.

He smiled gently at the confusion in my voice. "They leave some of their most important memories and some of their power to guide the next generation." He cleared his throat. "This was my father's. He left it for me before he was killed."

"Oh, Seth," I sobbed, guilt seeping into my skin at the fact that I had given something so precious to the warden, even if I hadn't known.

"It's okay," he soothed, gathering me in his arms and kissing the top of my head gently. He lifted my face up and brushed a soft, sparkling kiss on my lips that I felt all the way to my soul.

He surprised me then by stepping back and placing the crystal back in my hands. "I need you to keep it for now. They search my cell all the time. There's nowhere to hide anything in here. I'm afraid that it will be taken again if I try and keep it with me. Is there somewhere you can keep it safe?"

The guilt throbbed at me now, until my skin felt hot and tight. I still hadn't told him. Just a few weeks ago, I would have been the worst person to entrust the crystal with. He'd hate me as soon as he found out the truth. I'd have to tell him sometime, but not today. I didn't want to ruin today.

Everything was different now.

Before I could say anything, a guard hit the cell door, making us look guilty as we jumped apart like we'd done something wrong. I slipped the crystal back into my pocket and looked questioningly at the guard. Usually, they gave me more time with Seth than this.

"You have a visitor," he barked at Seth. I turned to look at Seth in surprise. As far as I knew, he hadn't gotten visitors the entire time I'd been in the prison. Seth's lips were pursed, and he looked deep in thought at the news.

"I'll just be going then," I told Seth. He nodded, distracted, sending me a small smile as I walked out.

I shot a look back at him before I turned the corner, but he wasn't watching me go like usual. Frowning and worrying about what kind of trouble a visitor meant for him, I doubled back and stayed just out of sight, waiting to see who his visitor was.

Seth wasn't allowed the privileges that other prisoners got, like being able to meet visitors in the waiting room where I'd met with my mother. So whoever his visitor was, they would be coming to his cell.

The sound of a woman's bell-like voice rang down the hallway and had me peeking around the corner to see who it was. My view of his cell was still blocked, so I crept closer, unsure what was up ahead.

And then I saw her. If Seth was the gleaming light fae with the features to match, she was his equal.

She had long, silver hair that reminded me of stardust, and even in the dim lighting and that far away, I could see that her eyes were an unusual shade of blue. Her skin was unmarred by a single blemish or freckle, and I somehow knew its golden tone was the exact tone Seth's would be had he not been tortured and starved on a daily basis.

The closeness between the two was obvious. She was standing just a few inches away from him, her hand on his chest. Considering Seth usually hated anyone touching him, the action bespoke of familiarity that had jealousy coursing through me. She was tall and slender, her forehead hitting just under his nose, despite the fact that Seth was well over six feet tall.

"Alania," he sighed. Was it my imagination that there was longing in the way he said her name? Had he said it with the same reverence that he'd said mine, just minutes before?

My jealousy grew thicker until I felt like I could drown in it.

"I've missed you," she told him in a voice so seductive, it could cause a priest to sin.

I hated her. I wanted to rip her hand off his chest.

For a second, his gaze seemed to meet mine, but I had to have imagined that, because when she stood up on her tiptoes to press her lips against his, he didn't stop her. Instead, he wrapped his arms around her and met her passionately, like he couldn't get enough.

My heart shattered into a million pieces. I couldn't take my eyes off of them.

"Guess old princey over there didn't tell you about his fiancée," a voice leered in my ear. Spinning around, I saw that one of the guards that frequently watched over Seth had managed to sneak up on me in the midst of my shocked heartbreak.

"Fiancée?" I asked, not comprehending what he was saying. I was still reeling from the kiss that was still happening behind me though. This all felt like some kind of nightmare. Was I going to wake up and find that I had dreamed this all along and I was still lying on my bed with Alaric?

"A little detail he must have missed when you were taking care of the bastard," the guard crowed.

My body felt overloaded, like I was going to burst out of my skin. I didn't stay to see anymore or hear anything more from the guard.

I just ran.

CHAPTER 13

SELENA

ears streamed down my face.

I didn't stop running, shoving past people, not giving a shit.

All I could picture in my mind was Seth and that extremely beautiful fae kissing him. What the hell was wrong with me to believe someone like him, a freaking royal, would really be interested in me? But I knew the answer, and as much as I hurt to admit to myself, it was the truth. I was the only company he had, so he latched onto me.

While I, the biggest idiot in the world, fell and let myself believe I meant something to him.

"Fuck!" I muttered, utterly outraged while my heart splintered.

And what was with the drawings of me? Were they a plot to make me believe he liked me? God, he kissed me, and I thought it meant the world. I shed tears for him, but maybe I was wrong. Maybe he was a liar and tricked everyone, and him being here was exactly what he deserved.

I'd done everything to help him, even had Alaric steal the stupid crystal in my pocket. We risked too much, only to discover that Seth wasn't really who he made himself out to be.

He tricked me, and now I felt like crap. Like I'd been run over by a truck and then it backed over me several times to make sure I was destroyed.

The image of him kissing her kept crashing into me, over and over, and I couldn't get it out of my mind. Neither could I ignore just how stunning she was... Here, I stood shorter than her, my hair limp, and orange was definitely not my color.

Who was I kidding? I didn't belong in their league, and Seth proved that royally today. Had he seen me? Had he been well aware I was watching him kiss that girl, and he just didn't care?

Asshole.

My chest squeezed tight, and I could barely breathe.

For a while, I'd started to think that Nightmare Penitentiary might not be that bad. I'd found myself with three men who made me feel special, who showed me how to love myself.

First, Keon hid the truth of his past from me, and I still didn't know what to make of him being a serial stalker, and capable of killing. At first, I assumed it was in self-defense, but I started to wonder if that wasn't the case after all.

Then, Seth showed his true colors about how he felt about me.

Bastards.

My body racked with sobs, I stumbled into a corner in the corridor with cells all around me and cried. I didn't care when the other prisoners hooted or laughed at me.

I let myself fall, and now it broke me. I cried in my hands, hating myself for getting so emotional, loathing Seth for using me.

Of course the fault was mine… Look where the hell I lived now. How could I trust anyone here?

"Hey, babe, you need some comfort?" a male's voice droned from in front of me. When his hand touched my arm, I jerked away and shook his touch off me.

"Don't touch me!" I managed as my eyes blurred behind tears.

I turned and kept running, not even remembering where I was headed, but I didn't want to stop or admit that I'd made a huge mistake.

This place wasn't that much different to real life, was it? Those outside these walls used me and saw me as a means to an end to benefit themselves, just like most inside here.

When I finally stopped running, I gasped for air and it took several moments to work out where I stood. Except this couldn't be right.

Ahead of me lay the corridor that took me to the warden's office, while somewhere behind me was the shrink's office.

My head hurt too much to make sense of how I got here without going through security. Except, I remembered when I first arrived at the prison, the walls at this institute shifted around as if it had a life of its own, opening up new passages.

The building had guided me here, and with that thought, Seth's crystal in my pocket suddenly felt heavy.

I stuck my hand into the pocket and curled the stone with curved edges over my fingers. This meant so much to him, but did Seth really deserve it?

My gaze lifted to the long stretch of the hallway ahead of me. Did I arrive here for a reason? I glanced around with my teary eyes, not seeing anyone around, and biting down on my lower lip, I made the decision to go speak with the warden.

I'd be honest with him and explain all I found out from Seth, which wasn't much, and say it was a lost cause. Returning the crystal, I could tell him to put me back on full time kitchen and delivery duty. That my time with Seth was wasted.

I swallowed the boulder in my throat, uncertainty clenching in my stomach. My stare remained locked on the corridor, but my feet hadn't moved yet.

He tricked me into liking him, I hated him a little more as I stood there battling with myself if I should end this with him.

Of course I should. He was a liar. He probably hadn't even been telling the truth about the importance of the crystal.

Distance was what I needed from Seth and Keon.

I marched ahead before I changed my mind, making my way toward the warden's office. I wiped away the tears that kept falling because I needed to be strong and not that girl who fell apart. Sure, I fucked up and let them fool me, but now I'd change things.

Outside his office stood two guards, large brutes, rigid and carrying tasers on their belts. Their presence sent goosebumps up my arms.

Several feet in front of me, the warden stepped out from a corridor and marched toward his office, and Alaric was right at his side. Neither of them saw me behind them, but my feet stopped working, and I froze on the spot.

Why was Alaric looking so chummy with the warden? They were talking like friends, and the warden even barked out a laugh.

What the hell?

I stiffened, but as the pair entered his office, I hurried forward to hear what in the world they were talking about.

Alaric never gave me the impression he was close with the warden. He'd gone so far as to warn me away from him.

One of the guards by his door stepped in my path. I craned my head up and offered him a smile. "I'm here to see the warden."

"Wait by the wall." His chin lifted in the direction farther down the hall.

I walked over and stood directly next to the door

and pressed my back to the wall and dug my hands into my pockets.

Then I lowered my head, ignoring the guard's glare, and tried to silence my hammering heart.

The hallway fell silent, and I strained my ears to listen to what was going on inside the office. The faint humming of voices sounded, but I needed to get closer.

This was the perfect moment for me to have some of the magic mojo from the shrink to have my out of my body experience.

Inching closer to the door, I bit the inside of my cheek, unsure how to get closer without draping myself over the door. Tilting my head to the side, pretending to be stretching, I caught a few words, but they remained garbled.

The guards started chatting in low whispers, something about boyfriend problems and how he found him cheating with his neighbor. As juicy as the story sounded, I shut out the voices and concentrated on what was going on in the room.

The deeper the guards got into their conversation, and turned their backs to me so I didn't overhear them, the more I gravitated closer to my own eavesdropping.

"I think I found it," the warden stated with conviction.

What in the world was he talking about? The seconds passed excruciatingly slow until Alaric responded.

"You sure about that? The fae hasn't given away anything you said, so how'd you track it down?"

My pulse jackhammered now where it rushed past my ears, deafening me for a few moments as I pieced everything together.

The warden had been searching for the stupid scepter, which was why he punished Seth, why he had me going in there to pry information out of him. But what did Alaric have to do with any of this?

His words from our last time together streamed over my mind.

If Seth says anything about the scepter, come to me before you say anything to the warden.

Heaviness dropped through me because I simply assumed he was worried about me getting in trouble. Except he was fishing for information. Did he want the scepter for himself? What the hell was the big deal with this stupid artifact?

It didn't really matter now, did it?

Apparently, Alaric had been hiding secrets from me too. He was using me to get it all for himself.

Betrayal flared over me, twisting my insides into knots. My mouth fell open, but I held back the gasp wanting to escape.

I snapped back to the wall when the guards glanced my way. But I couldn't stay here a second longer, so I pushed away from the hall when the guard moved with tremendous speed.

"Where are you going?"

"I-I'll come back and see the warden later. He seems busy. Will you please walk me back to the prison sector?"

He grumbled but nodded, and I followed behind him, my stomach twisting on itself.

There was no one I could trust, and until I worked out what was going on, I was holding onto the crystal.

I'd never felt so vulnerable in my whole life. And that was saying a lot, considering everything I'd gone through. A sense of betrayal tightened over my chest.

Three men who I cared for, maybe even loved. It had all been a ruse.

They lied to me.

Hid secrets.

Used me.

I dragged myself forward and didn't even look back once the guard escorted me past the main door that led out of the office sector. I broke into a run. My throat thickened, and the tears came again. I rubbed them away, but it made no difference. I wanted the world to open up and swallow me.

They used sex to lure me, and I felt victim because I was scared and lonely.

I needed to pull myself together and stand up for myself. No one else would do that but me.

I was a strong woman, and if I survived this far, then I could face anything thrown at me. Then why couldn't I stop crying? Why did my chest feel like it just shattered into shards of glass? I choked on a sob and wasn't even paying attention to where I was going. This area seemed darker, and for those few seconds, I swore I'd made my way back to the seedy area near Alaric's cell.

Someone snagged my arm from behind me, drawing me to stop.

"Selena," Keon said. "What are you doing here alone?"

I spun and came face to face with him. My mouth dried because when I looked at him, all I saw were the newspaper articles.

"Why are you crying, baby. Did someone hurt you?"

I ripped my hand from his grasp because everything was too much. "Don't. Just leave me alone."

Confusion flashed over his face, and he stepped closer, standing in my personal space, grabbing hold of my arm. "What's going on? Talk to me."

The color from his cheeks drained, and his eyes looked like glass cracking, dread curling behind them. His stiffened posture told the story of someone who responded with fury.

This gorgeous man I'd fallen for, who I picked up from a pub, was a real serial stalker. I'd fucked myself really well, hadn't I?

"I can't help if you don't talk to me," he persisted. "Is it about what we did before?"

I shook my head. "No, I don't want to talk about this right now." When I wrenched my hand from him that time, I stumbled backward, and he lunged to catch me.

"Fuck, Selena. Are you going to freak out on me, because that's going to mess me up on the inside. If someone else hurt you, I'll make them regret it."

His words grasped my heart as a mini battle took

place within me, pulling me in two directions. An ache flared over my chest as I realized he feared losing me. Except right now, I just needed time alone to sort out my confused thoughts. "Please, not now," I murmured.

Shock grasped his expression, and for those few moments, we stared at each other as though we were strangers. My heart stopped working from the ache of how much Keon meant to me, but fuck... Too many things were happening at once. It was too much to take, and it took everything I had to hold myself together and not crumble to the ground.

"Hey, the girl said to leave her alone," a deep guttural voice I recognized barked. It was Laz, the hellhound shifter I'd bumped into a couple of times.

He meant well by coming to my rescue, but this was the worst time to butt in.

I inhaled and managed to say, "It's okay, Laz."

Keon's mouth curled into a grimace. "You know this dickhead?"

"Hey." The hellhound shoved a meaty palm into Keon's side, but he didn't budge, and instead, jerked his head to the intruder.

"Touch me again, and I'll rip your spine out." His voice was a growl, and sounded nothing like the Keon I'd known.

But had I ever known the real him?

With a grunt, Keon shuddered, and he seemed to change, his eyes darkening. Were there horns extending out from his temples?

The fuck!

A growl spilled from his mouth, a wisp of black smoke curling out from the corners of his mouth.

I flinched, my body trembling as he lunged at Laz.

Then all hell broke loose.

CHAPTER 14

SELENA

My heart couldn't take this.

Too much had happened already... too damn much that now I stood paralyzed, trying to make sense of what exactly I was watching.

Keon seemed different, and I couldn't work it out.

But Laz wasn't backing down either. They came together in a thunderous clash, Keon surprisingly powerful. He locked the hellhound shifter's head in an arm lock, his fist slamming in his head.

"Stop!" I yelled. I didn't need this on my conscience along with everything else. I rushed up to them and grabbed his uniform at his back, tugging it. "Keon, fucking stop this."

But he didn't hear me at first, roaring, while Laz hurled his fist into his Keon's side. This was insane.

I frantically looked around at anyone watching the fight to help. But their greedy smiles, their hoots were the opposite of someone who'd stop the show.

"Keon, please!" I pleaded. "This is between us. I'll talk to you, just leave him alone."

That time, he glanced at me, the fiery mask of rage he wore slipped away.

"Let him go, Keon. Please."

It took several moments for him to finally nod and release his hold over Laz. "Selena," he said, his voice drowning in sorrow.

But that window of time was all it took for Laz to slip free and swing back around. The glint of something in his hand caught my attention.

He gripped a small blade, his knuckles white from how tight he held the weapon, his face red with fury.

I screamed and lunged forward just as Laz drove the blade right into Keon's gut.

I froze, while Keon bellowed and clutched his stomach. My hands went to Keon's injury, my eyes locked on the blood. So much dripped out, the red stain on his uniform around the stab wound spreading outward.

Keon shoved me away and wrenched the weapon free before tossing it in the opposite direction, almost missing a bystander who ducked at the last second.

Terror closed in around my chest. "Keon?"

He trembled horribly, and panic clawed at my chest. I clutched his arm, needing to take him to the infirmary.

Except something was wrong. His hand felt like fire under my fingers. His body seemed to twitch, just as I'd seen shifters do before they transformed.

I lifted my gaze to him for a second as he looked my

way, and he wasn't himself, darkness swallowing every inch of white in his eyes.

"Get away from me, Selena. Run!" he growled, and pushed a hand into my shoulder.

I stumbled backward, my heart banging against my rib cage. What was going on?

There was a grunt from Laz, while Keon transformed right before my eyes. Hands lengthened into clawed tips. His boots split, tearing apart and falling away into shreds as hooves pushed free. All the while, black horns pushed out from his temples.

I gasped.

Oh. My. God. I'd been sleeping with a demon.

The crowd made oohing sounds, like this fascinated them. Except, I was freaking out. I had no clue Keon was anything but human.

He changed into something dark.

Why didn't I know this about him? But how could I when he didn't even tell me about his stalker past? Nobody was who they said they were in this prison. Nobody but foolish me, who wore her heart on her sleeve. I was a naïve sucker, apparently.

Keon swung toward Laz and slammed into him, both of these men were mountains. They crashed to the floor, sending the whole corridor into a trembling quake.

Holy crap!

My back hit a wall, and I gasped for each breath. Laz's body trembled ferociously, and if it wasn't for the spell in this prison, I didn't doubt he'd be a full-blown hellhound by now.

Punches flew in every direction, the growls were demonic and flooded the air.

So many more inmates rushed over to watch the commotion. It wouldn't be long before the guards arrived, and nothing would be the same again.

Laz shoved Keon off him, sending him right into someone's cell door, breaking it open, and he crashed inside.

Someone yelled from the surprise entrance. But it didn't take long for Keon to climb to his feet and re-emerge.

I didn't recognize this man. He stood taller, broader, with his fucking horns and hoofed feet. And smoke twirled out from his flaring nostrils.

He stepped forward, his chest heaving for breath, in and out, his eyes completely black.

How could I not have sensed this in him before?

I expelled a long breath.

Laz leapt to his feet, the two powerhouses facing each other off while bystanders cheered, calling for them to fight, fight, fight.

Except, what was going down here was my fault.

Laz snarled and pulled away from Keon for a sliver of a moment. But Keon never stopped, he threw himself at his opponent like a madman, grunting.

They barreled toward me, and the thump of punches and claws tearing each other apart was too much. Laz fought with everything while pinned under Keon.

"Enough!" I shouted, frustrated and furious. I'd put up with so much in this place. And with Keon's aggression, it wouldn't be long before he killed Laz.

Panic rose inside me, it came in an instant. So I lashed out and grabbed Keon's arm before he did more damage and ended up inside these walls as an inmate instead of a guard.

He twisted around, his cold, black eyes on me. Dropping Laz from his grasp, he spun abruptly, coming right for me.

I shoved myself backward, my hands stuck out to stop him. "Keon, what are you doing?"

But the person looking at me wasn't Keon. This was whatever lived inside him staring at me, and now, it saw me as a meal.

I'd been so wrong. So fucking wrong to think I held any sway in this aggressive fight. A terrified cry escaped past my lips, and I pushed away. The crowd parted, doing nothing to help.

In a flash, Keon attacked me, his hand lashed out, clawed fingers tearing across my throat.

He ripped my life away in an instant.

My knees fell out from under me, and I collapsed. I weakly grasped my throat, but the blood seeped out between my fingers until I was kneeling in a pool of blood.

Everything was going dark so fast, my breaths gurgled with each raspy intake of air.

Shadows moved all around me, voices that made no sense. I could hear screams.

But none of that mattered anymore.

Death was coming for me. I felt myself slip away. Everything I'd done brought me to this spot, where I'd lost everything.

I should be furious, but instead, a strange calmness settled over me as my world faded away. And all I could think about was knowing that despite how horrific my existence had been, for a short period of time, I'd thought I experienced the kind of bliss and heartfelt love I only dreamed about.

Three men who lied to me, who betrayed me, who used me… They'd given me a gift, and then they'd taken it away.

It had all been an illusion, a disappointment, like everything else in my life.

At least death would give me an escape.

The world turned black, and I took my last breath.

My death was swift.

ABOUT MILA YOUNG

**Find all Mila young books at
www.milayoungbooks.com**

Best-selling author, Mila Young tackles everything
with the zeal and bravado of the fairytale heroes she
grew up reading about. She slays monsters, real and
imaginary, like there's no tomorrow. By day she rocks a
keyboard as a marketing extraordinaire. At night she
battles with her mighty pen-sword, creating fairytale
retellings, and sexy ever after tales. In her spare time,
she loves pretending she's a mighty warrior, walks on
the beach with her dogs, cuddling up with her cats, and
devouring every fantasy tale she can get her pinkies on.

Ready to read more and more from Mila Young?
www.subscribepage.com/milayoung

Join Mila's **Wicked Readers group** for exclusive
content, latest news, and giveaway.
**www.facebook.com/
groups/milayoungwickedreaders**

For more information...

milayoungauthor@gmail.com

ABOUT C.R. JANE

A Texas girl living in Utah now, I'm a wife, mother, lawyer, and now author. My stories have been floating around in my head for years, and it has been a relief to finally get them down on paper. I'm a huge Dallas Cowboys fan and I primarily listen to Beyonce and Taylor Swift...don't lie and say you don't too.

My love of reading started probably when I was three and with a faster than normal ability to read, I've devoured hundreds of thousands of books in my life. It only made sense that I would start to create my own worlds since I was always getting lost in others'.

I like heroines who have to grow in order to become badasses, happy endings, and swoon-worthy, devoted, (and hot) male characters. If this sounds like you, I'm pretty sure we'll be friends.

I'm so glad to have you on my team...check out the links below for ways to hang out with me and more of my books you can read!

**Join my Facebook readers' group:
www.facebook.com/groups/C.R.FatedRealm/**

Visit my website: www.crjanebooks.com/

www.ingramcontent.com/pod-product-compliance
Lightning Source LLC
Chambersburg PA
CBHW020803190726
48285CB00006B/2149